Kiki's

MEMOIRS

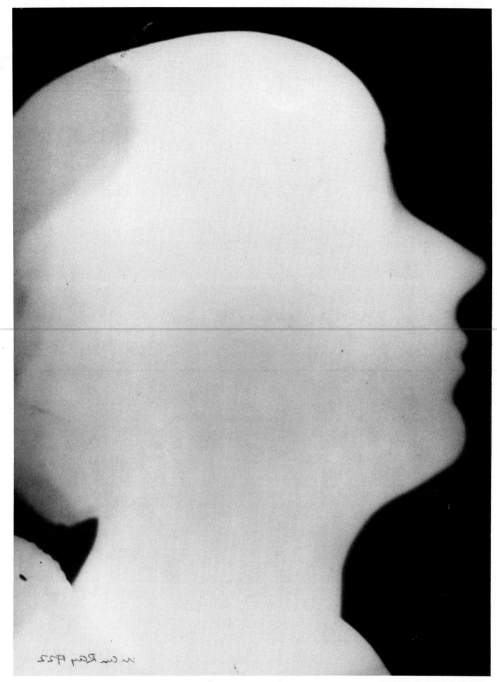

Photo Man Ray

RAYOGRAPH, 1922

Kiki's
MEMOIRS

Introductions by *Ernest Hemingway*
and *Foujita* • Reproductions of
Paintings by *Kiki* • Photography
by *Man Ray* • Translated from the
French by *Samuel Putnam* •
Additional Material Translated by
Billy Klüver and Julie Martin •
Edited, Annotated and with a
Foreword by *Billy Klüver and
Julie Martin*

THE ECCO PRESS

For Göran Ohlin, who also took on the work with humor.

THE ECCO PRESS
100 West Broad Street
Hopewell, New Jersey 08525
Published simultaneously in Canada by
Penguin Books Canada Ltd., Ontario
Printed in the United States of America

Library of Congress Cataloging-in-Publication Data
Kiki, 1901 – 1953.
     Kiki's memoirs / introduction by Ernest Hemingway and Foujita ; reproductions of paintings by Kiki ; photography by Man Ray ; translated from the French by Samuel Putnam ; additional material translated by Billy Klüver and Julie Martin ; edited and annotated by Billy Klüver and Julie Martin.
          p.   cm.
     ISBN 0-88001-496-2
     1. Kiki, 1901 – 1953. 2. Artist's models—France—Paris—Biography. 3. Montparnasse (Paris, France)—History—20th century.   I. Klüver, Billy, 1927– . II. Martin, Julie. III. Title.
N7574.5.F8K55   1996
709'.2—dc20
[B]   96-27746

The text of this book is set in Lanston Caslon 337

9 8 7 6 5 4 3 2 1

FIRST ECCO EDITION

CONTENTS

Photo Man Ray

IN MAN RAY'S APARTMENT, RUE LA CONDAMINE, 1921

FOREWORD

Billy Klüver with Julie Martin

I first heard about Kiki when I saw her in Fernand
Léger's film, *Ballet Mécanique*, which I showed at the
Film Society at the University in Stockholm in 1949.
A knowledgeable friend informed me that Kiki was fa-
mous for not having any pubic hair.

Thirty years later Julie Martin and I decided to
develop a mini-series for television based on historical
material from France, whose rich cultural heritage
had not appeared on American television, as had the
minutiae of British life and imperial history in a BBC
presentation. We first thought of focusing on Anaïs
Nin's life in Paris. I spent time in Montparnasse, be-

gan to read some of the memoirs of the 1920s, and realized that Kiki should be our real focus.

Kiki appeared in virtually every book from the period and was featured in the memoirs of artists and writers who had made Montparnasse their home, like Man Ray, Brassai, Djuna Barnes, Robert McAlmon and Kay Boyle, Morley Callaghan, and of course Ernest Hemingway. The thousands of tourists who descended on Montparnasse in the late 1920s spread her fame beyond the borders of France; as French critic André Salmon announced, "Kiki is known from San Francisco to Oslo!"

Kiki, the best-known and best-loved woman in Montparnasse, was still remembered in the 1980s; when I mentioned her name, people who had known her would fling out their hands in a classic French gesture, smile and sigh, "Ah, Kiki!"

By then I knew she had written her memoirs, but how to find them? I walked into Shakespeare and Company off quai de Montebello and asked the elderly lady sitting by the desk for a copy of *Kiki Sou-*

venirs. She looked me over and told me to come back the next day. When I returned, she took the book from underneath her table and, with the gravity of passing on the Holy Grail, admonished me, "This is my only copy. Don't ever sell it." Since then only a few more copies have come to our attention, each of them with an exuberant dedication by Kiki on the flyleaf. Juliet Man Ray showed me the English edition of *Kiki's Memoirs*, carefully preserved in the studio on rue Férou that Juliet shared with Man Ray until his death in 1976.

In search of Kiki's roots, we went to Châtillon-sur-Seine with Kiki's best friend, Thérèse Treize, and looked for a stone house with a wooden spiral staircase that Treize remembered from her visits there in the 1920s. Finally we went to the local bar, which is the method I used to find traces of people in Paris. Neighborhoods change slowly in France. We started talking to the patron Henri, who had gone to school with Kiki. He told us that some relative of the Prin family lived not far away on rue de Cygne. Much of

Châtillon had been destroyed by Italian bombing in World War II, but this section of the old town had survived since the Middle Ages. We immediately went there, knocked on a door in an ancient stone wall at No. 11, over the top of which we could see the outdoor wooden staircase. When we showed the photo of Kiki's grandmother to the old lady who answered, she immediately said, "C'est ma grandmère." It was Madeleine, the red-headed cousin Kiki writes about so lovingly in her memoirs. Now 78 years old, and having lost her husband and daughter, she was living in the same house that Kiki's grandmother had occupied since the 1920s. She was just finishing Sunday lunch with Claude, her live-in boyfriend, forty years younger than she, who made his living carving sculptures for gravestones.

We visited Madeleine often, sitting with her and Claude in a room crammed with two stoves, a refrigerator, an oilcloth-covered dining table, a couch bed, a television set, and a bureau in one corner with photos of her husband, her daughter, and Kiki. Over tradi-

A POSE IN AN INFORMAL SESSION WITH MAN RAY

tional meals of rabbit stew, she talked about Kiki and herself growing up in Châtillon in a rapid-fire Burgundian dialect that was hard to follow, even for the French friends who came with us.

Our artist friend Annie Tolleter followed the trail of Kiki's ancestors in the records of the *mairies* in the small towns around Châtillon and helped us put together Kiki's genealogy.

Kiki was born in Châtillon-sur-Seine, in the Côte d'Or section of Burgundy, site of the Source de la Douix, one of the springs feeding the Seine. The town sits next to a large forest and on the edge of the Plateau de Langres. In 1900 the population was just under 5,000.

We traced the Prin family back three generations to Bourg-St.-Maurice in the Savoie, where Pierre François Prin served in Napoleon's lancers and then became a shepherd. The family followed the slow migration of sheep husbandry to the area around Châtillon-sur-Seine, where the men married local women. Sheepherding eventually died out, so Kiki's grandfather became a laborer building and repairing roads. He married Marie Esprit in 1870 and settled in Châtillon. Kiki's mother, Marie Ernestine Prin, was born in 1883, the fourth of five children. She worked as a linotypist for a local newspaper. She fell in love with Maxime Legros, a coal and charcoal merchant ten years her senior, and had her first child—who died at birth—when she was sixteen. The next year she gave birth to a daughter, Maxmilliene Alice, who died after four months. Kiki was born a year and a half later in October 1901 and christened Alice Ernestine Prin, taking her mother's family name, as her father did not legally recognize her.

A large part of the memoirs is the story of Kiki's adolescence in Paris with its sexual awakenings and traps. Prostitution was the common fate of most young unskilled unmarried girls from the country. Even those who found work as domestics, seamstresses, laundresses, or other menial jobs, were paid wages so low that many turned to part-time prostitution to survive. The economics of prostitution were such that on average every Frenchman in Paris enjoyed one *passe* every day. Kiki's wit and intelligence saved her from becoming entangled in prostitution, and her natural attraction to the artists' community in Montparnasse provided her with a safe home.

In the late 19th century artists started leaving Montmartre, which began to be overrun by bars, nightclubs, and cabarets with overpriced champagne, nude dancing and more if you knew where to find it, accompanied inevitably by prostitution and petty crime. The artists were attracted to the peace and tranquility of Montparnasse, which was essentially a bourgeois residential neighborhood. There was no night life or prostitution. Also Montparnasse had become a boom area for the building of artists' studios in the deep courtyards of ordinary apartment buildings. These studios were not subject to building codes and were often flimsy, badly heated and sometimes built from leftover materials from the recurrent World's Fairs in Paris. The intensive café life that developed in Montparnasse had as one of its compo-

KIKI SIMPLY SLID HER DRESS DOWN

nents the desire of artists to flee their cold, unheated studios when darkness made it impossible to work any longer.

Since the days of Louis XIV, it was the cultural policy of the French state to encourage artists to live and work in Paris. During the 1920s the government adopted a special attitude toward Montparnasse. Criminal elements were never allowed to take root there, and the police deliberately kept a low profile. The artists' community was considered a "free zone," and more eccentric behavior was permitted there than was tolerated in other areas of Paris. The artists left their mark on life in Montparnasse.

Freedom and experimentation permeated all aspects of life in Montparnasse. Those who came there were free to realize themselves—artistically, intellectually, politically, and sexually. It was an aristocracy of the individual, and the supreme individual was Kiki. Alone, and by force of her own personality, she brought herself from the lowest class of society, from dire poverty, to become one of the most visible personalities in the artists' community in the years between the two world wars.

Kiki's natural creativity flourished in the permissive atmosphere of Montparnasse. She modeled for the artists—Kisling and Foujita, Per Krohg, and Alexander Calder, among others. But Kiki was more a friend of the painters than a professional model.

She was well on her way to becoming a star when Man Ray met her in the fall of 1921. Their eight-year love affair, from 1921 to 1929, was one of the longest and most celebrated in Montparnasse. Kiki loved him unreservedly, as we can see in a letter she wrote him from Châtillon, where she had to go to visit her family during the first months of their love affair:

"I have a heavy heart when I think that tonight you will be alone in your bed, because I would like to put you beddy-bye myself so that you could snuggle up in my arms. I love you too much, . . . you are not made to be loved, you are too calm. . . . But I have to take you as you are, you are, after all, my lover, whom I adore, who will make me die of pleasure, of sorrow, and of love. . . . I bite your mouth until it bleeds, and I'm getting drunk on your indifferent, sometimes even mean, look. Until Monday big darling Your KikiadoresyouMan."

And with her usual burst of humor Kiki could charm as well, "You shouldn't complain because you have one of the most beautiful little women of the Rotonde, not dumb, in love, not boring, not a woman of luxury, not a whore and not syphilitic (a little wonder)."

Kiki worked with Man Ray in more than forty photographic sessions from 1921 into the early 1930s and their collaboration produced some of the greatest Surrealist images of the 1920s. It is rare in the history of photography for an artist to work with one model so intensively: Alfred Stieglitz and Georgia O'Keefe or Robert Mapplethorpe and Lisa Lyon come to mind. Man Ray captured the multifaceted beauty of Kiki. Clothed, the fashions took on her sensuality. Nude, she presented her body without embarrassment. Her breasts were perfect and she knew it. Her hips expressed comfort and ease, and her poses were never stereotyped or obvious. It's a world of sensuality and delight.

She starred in three of Man Ray's experimental films: *Retour à la Raison*, *Emak Bakia*, and *Etoile de Mer*, as well as Léger's *Ballet Mécanique*, and appeared in three commercial silent films: *Galerie des Monstres*, directed by Jaque Catelain, *La Capitaine Jaune* by the Danish director Anders-Wilhelm Sandberg, and *Cette Vieille Canaille* by Anton Litvak.

She was the star attraction at the artists' nightclub, The Jockey, which opened in 1923. In the late '20s she performed at other Montparnasse nightclubs, as well as at Le Boeuf sur le Toit, the chic and fashionable club on the right bank frequented by successful artists and writers and members of Paris society.

For performing at The Jockey, Treize made her layers of full, loose underskirts that floated as she moved, which Kiki often pulled up far enough to reveal that she was wearing nothing underneath. Jacqueline Goddard, one of her friends whom we interviewed extensively, described Kiki singing: "She would lower her head, moving it from side to side. All her movements were economical and rounded; she made a light dance with her hips, very slow and almost imperceptible. She always wore a shawl which she slid over her shoulders as if to say, 'It's not so bad, what I'm singing here.' She performed her outrageously dirty songs in a way that offended no one." Her trademark song was an old folk tune for which the Surrealist poet Robert Desnos had written new words: 'The young girls of Camaret say they are all virgins,/ But when they are in my bed they prefer my tool/ more than a candle/ more than a candle. . . .''

She began to paint in a cheerful naive style, primarily scenes of her childhood in Châtillon, idealized landscapes, and portraits of her friends. An exhibition of her paintings was organized at Galerie au Sacre du Printemps in 1927. Robert Desnos wrote an evocative preface to her catalogue, and Kiki presided with majesty at the crowded opening party. The Paris *Tribune* reported that the opening "brought out the habitués of the Quarter en masse. From five o'clock until after midnight they came in a steady stream, and the little gallery seethed with excited comments. It

Photo Man Ray

CREATED BY A SINGLE FLOODLIGHT,
KIKI'S SHADOW TAKES ON A LIFE OF ITS OWN

was, so far as we know, the most successful *vernissage* of the year. Those who came to smile, remained to buy and before the night was over, a large number of the canvasses were decorated with little white *vendu* [sold] cards." Kiki had another exhibition of her work at Galerie Georges Bernheim in December of 1930.

Henri Broca, a journalist and caricaturist from Bordeaux, came to Paris around 1925 and worked for various newspapers as an illustrator. High-strung and full of energy, he fell in love with a dream, the dream of Montparnasse. He saw Kiki as the embodiment of this dream, and he fell in love with her too.

Broca first published a 42-page book that celebrated Montparnasse, in which he combined caricatures of Kiki, Man Ray, Foujita, and several Montparnasse barmen with lively interviews and comments about Montparnasse, topped off with full-page ads that he drew for eight of the leading night spots, from Le Dôme and La Rotonde to the newly opened College Inn and La Cigogne. The title echoed Cocteau's cry of years before, "T'en fais pas! Viens à Montparnasse!" (Don't hesitate! Come to Montparnasse!)

They didn't hesitate, and they did come to Montparnasse. It was said that you could buy a ticket in Des Moines direct to Le Dôme. Thousands of tourists from America as well as from Germany, England, and Scandinavia passed through Montparnasse each week. A drink at Le Dôme and dancing at the Coupole was as mandatory as a look at the Venus de Milo. Mostly the artists ignored the tourists.

In February 1929, Broca started a magazine called *Paris-Montparnasse*, and by this time he and Kiki, who had been drifing away from Man Ray for some time, were living together. Broca mixed nostalgic stories of life in Montparnasse with gossipy items on the comings and goings of the artist as celebrity. Broca glorified the old days of Montparnasse, but he promoted the new Montparnasse, where the "industry of pleasure" and "commerce of drinks" had taken over.

Above all, Broca celebrated Kiki. The biggest event he organized was a performance afternoon in

May 1929 to raise money for poor artists at the Bobino Theatre on rue de la Gaieté. All the artists and friends that Kiki writes about in the last part of her memoirs took part: Pascin designed the program which was signed and numbered in a limited edition; Foujita performed with a dummy of himself; Treize and the Montparnasse Girls performed the cancan; Marie Vassilieff danced Russian traditional dances; and as the main attraction, Kiki performed her bawdy songs. The climax of the event was the election of Kiki as "Queen of Montparnasse." A sensual photograph of Kiki with a rose in her teeth taken that day was said to have been made into a postcard that sold 100,000 copies.

Both Man Ray and Edward Titus, the husband of Helena Rubinstein who established a rare-book store and small publishing house in Montparnasse, take credit for encouraging Kiki to write her memoirs, but it was Broca who helped her finish her manuscript and who published the first chapters in the April 1929 issue of *Paris-Montparnasse*, announcing that "Kiki

KIKI, *PASTORAL*, 1925

has written her memoirs, which in the near future will be published by editions de *Paris-Montparnasse*." We found the contract Kiki signed with Broca on April 24 to publish her manuscript entitled *Kiki*, in a deluxe, signed edition of two hundred copies and in a regular edition. The expenses of publication and publicity would be paid from the first sales; after that Kiki and Broca would share the proceeds.

On June 25 Broca organized a book-signing party at the newly opened Falstaff Restaurant. "To the sound of champagne corks popping, Kiki signed her book," Broca reported in *Paris-Montparnasse*. Another book signing, at Edouard Loewy's bookshop on October 26, was covered by the Paris *Tribune:* "Kiki was kissing all comers last Saturday night. The line formed about 9 o'clock outside of a bookshop on boulevard Raspail. When the news swept the Quarter that for 30 francs one could get a copy of Kiki's *Memoirs*, her autograph, and a kiss in the bargain, men forgot their *demis*, dates and dignity, and scampered over."

In 1929 Titus had just published D.H. Lawrence's *Lady Chatterley's Lover* and happily agreed to publish the English version of *Kiki Souvenirs*. He turned to the American journalist Samuel Putnam to make the English translation, and he asked Ernest Hemingway to write an introduction. As a favor to Kiki, Hemingway agreed.

Hemingway's challenge in his introduction, that "It is a crime to translate it," stirred up a storm of protest from Putnam and Titus that livened up—and greatly lengthened—the forewords to the *Memoirs*.

Bennett Cerf, chief editor of Random House, was in Paris on business in June 1930, where he had just signed a contract with André Gide to publish his autobiography. Titus showed him the first unbound pages off the press of *Kiki's Memoirs*, and they were discussing the possibility of Cerf acquiring the book for Random House in America. But Cerf had to leave Paris before anything could be agreed upon. In early July, Cerf ordered one hundred-fifty copies at two dollars each, and Titus quickly shipped them to New

York on July 22. However, Kiki's reputation had preceded her, and on August 22 Cerf wrote Titus, "As we gravely feared, the shipment of *Kiki's Memoirs* was held up by the U.S. Customs." Cerf asked Titus to mail small anonymous packages of fifteen books each, valued at less than one hundred dollars, to ten Random House editors and employees whose home addresses he listed.

An American journalist in Paris learned that Customs had seized her book and immediately went to tell Kiki: "The village queen was informed of the bad news yesterday while sharing a cracker with her little Peky on the terrace of the Coupole. Laconically and with a characteristic shrug, she remarked: "I am not losing any weight over it.""

Bennett Cerf was more concerned. When Titus wrote that he could only send packages weighing 5 pounds or less, which meant three books at a time, Cerf wrote back, "I am counting on getting at least 50 Kiki from you by mail, so for the love of heaven, don't disappoint me on this." And a month later he wrote again, "I am hoping that you have mailed at least a few of them to me privately since there are a few people whose orders we are particularly anxious to fill on this book."

I don't know how many copies got into the country that way or how many were brought back by happy tourists who were able to smuggle in their copies of the book with Kiki's amusing dedications. I do know that in 1933 James Joyce's *Ulysses* was declared to be not obscene and was "admitted into the United States," *Lady Chatterley's Lover* was taken off the Postmaster General's list in 1959, and in 1964 the Supreme Court ruled that Henry Miller's *Tropic of Cancer* was not pornographic; but as late as the 1970s, when I found *Kiki's Memoirs* in the card catalogue at New York Public Library and requested it, it was still held in a section for banned books and had to be read in a separate room.

While *Kiki's Memoirs* are as open, honest, and forthright as Kiki herself, they would hardly make any publisher think twice about accepting them today. But there is one book Kiki was part of that would. Man Ray and poets Benjamin Peret and Louis Aragon published *1929*, which contained four graphic, erotic photographs titled "The Four Seasons" and poems in the form of nursery rhymes but using crude barracks-room language and humor to describe the months of the year. Man Ray, the eternal *bricoleur*, rigged his camera to obtain unprecedented close-up images of Kiki and himself making love. While they are more esthetic than pornographic, they didn't pass the French censors in 1929 and are still too revealing to be printed in this edition of her *Memoirs*.

Kiki and Broca had a passionate but stormy love affair. One of its better moments was reported in the local Paris *Tribune* gossip column: "Bulletin: Two friends, walking along the boulevard, entertained each other and the rest of the promenaders with an endurance kiss. It started near the Falstaff and held until they came in front of the Coupole bar, where they were greeted by the little flower girl. Broca bought a flower, pinned it, and he and Kiki went inside." But

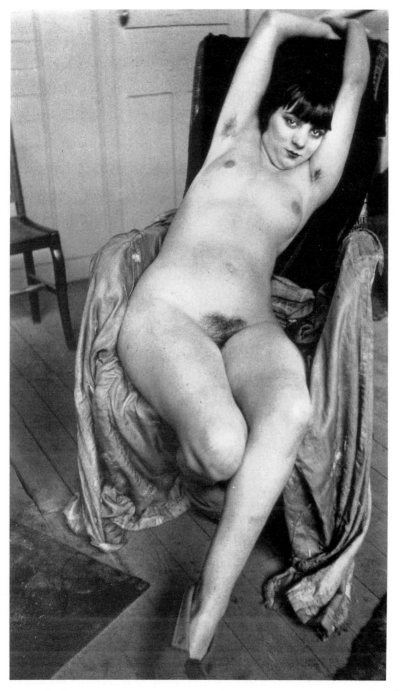

Photo Man Ray

LOOKING

soon after final plans had been made for this edition of *Kiki's Memoirs*, Henri Broca began to exhibit eccentric and violent behavior; Kiki had to commit him to St. Anne's Hospital, where she visited him often.

The worldwide depression, sparked by the Wall Street Crash in 1929, settled on Montparnasse, and Kiki began to sing full-time in boîtes and cabarets to make a living. Broca did reappear in Montparnasse, with plans to publish a guidebook to the eating places in the Quarter. He managed to put out a last issue of *Paris Montparnasse* in 1933. But after several relapses, he went to convalesce with his family in Bordeaux, where he died in 1935.

In the cabarets Kiki met André Laroque, a tax collector who played the accordion and piano to make extra money. Laroque soon quit his day job and accompanied Kiki full time. They appeared at all the new cabarets in Montparnasse and performed at private parties and occasionally at Right Bank music halls. Kiki still performed at The Jockey, but she had moved full-time into the world of Parisian nightlife.

In 1950 Kiki wrote three autobiographical articles for a Paris newspaper, which we have translated and included in this edition. While they paint a somewhat more somber picture of her childhood and early days in Paris, the language has the earthiness and amusing turns of phrase that give even the most harrowing stories a feeling of peasant endurance and unfailing gaiety. Like the *Memoirs*, these articles have the flavor of sitting with Kiki at a table, on the *terrasse* of Le Dôme, enjoying her nonstop stories about the vicissitudes of her life.

Through it all Kiki remained Kiki. She often told Laroque, "My dear, all I need is an onion, a bit of bread, and a bottle of red, and I will always find somebody to offer me that." That somebody was Laroque; he lived with Kiki until her death in 1953.

I met Laroque briefly just before he died, by sitting at La Rotonde with Jill Krauskopf, who did much of the early research on Kiki with us. We started talking loudly about Kiki. Mme. Vacher, who had owned the O.K. nightclub where Kiki sang in the 1930s, approached me. She took me to meet André Laroque, who still lived at No. 2 rue Bréa in the same apartment he had shared with Kiki, which was still filled with her paintings. He told me that Kiki was as lively as ever when she died. Coming back from a weekend with friends in the country, she collapsed by the small statue on the triangular square at the corner of rue Bréa, rue Vavin, and rue Nôtre Dame des Champs. She died March 23, 1953. In addition to many stories in French newspapers and magazines, a short obituary appeared in the *New York Times*, and *Life* magazine ran a three-page story in December of that year: "Artists loved to paint her not only because she had a fascinating catlike face and a voluptuous body, but because she always seemed gay. . . . She wore her black hair alternately straight or in curls, changed the color of her eye shadow to match her dress and changed the contour of her pencilled eyebrows to match her mood." *Life* ends its tribute to her

KIKI, *SUNDAY*, 1924

by quoting an old friend who remembered that, "We laughed, mon dieu, how we laughed."

Kiki always had a ready comeback, a pun or a joke. When art dealer Julien Levy declined to sleep with her, she shot back, punning in two languages, "Tu n'es pas un homme, mais un hommelette!" (You're not a man, but a man-lette!) She was always the center of a group of laughing people, whom she would keep entertained for hours with her improbable stories and tantalizing wit. Although her language was sometimes vulgar, she never used it derisively, and it never offended her listeners. Journalists writing about Montparnasse always noted that a place perked up when Kiki arrived.

Kiki was a star of everyday life. She was a true child of nature, who acted spontaneously and impulsively. "Never again," she once cried to Man Ray, "will Kiki do the identical same thing three days running, never, never, never!" Provocative and uninhibited, she took lovers as she wished, but was loyal and generous. On the spur of the moment, she would show her breasts or lift her skirts in a bar or restaurant, telling the delighted patrons, "That will cost you a franc or two," and then turn over the money to a needy friend.

I once shared a taxi from the American Hospital in Paris with a French doctor. When he saw *Kiki's Memoirs* in my hand, he told me that shortly before Kiki's death she used to come regularly to his hospital and pass around candy to the elderly patients. I thought the story was remarkable, not only for her unfailing generosity, but because she herself had little money toward the end of her life. She stayed true to the personality she had forged in the carefree days of Montparnasse.

Kiki remains the embodiment of the outspokenness, audacity, and creativity that marked this period of Montparnasse, which as the French writer Jules Romaine has said, "was without peer or parallel, a moment in time forever lost, but never forgotten."

KIKI'S PORTRAIT OF FOUJITA, APRIL 1923

MY FRIEND KIKI

Foujita

Winter—Kiki envelopes his glory in a superb gray beard. At night he is surrounded by thousands of fashionable people in his sumptuous mansion .

Summer—Kiki, next to two playing boys, smokes his pipe and dreams at his villa in the Midi.

Summer and winter, Kiki never wears any underpants, day and night every minute, she thinks only about eating.

Three Kikis: Kiki Van Dongen, Kiki Kisling, Kiki Kiki are world-famous celebrities and truly delightful.

It was a long time ago when Kiki Kiki came to my studio to pose for the first time, in reality it was not a studio, but a simple garage where I lived. She came in slowly and timidly, her cute little finger held up to her small red mouth, swinging her behind confidently. When she took off her coat, she was absolutely naked, a small handkerchief, in lively colors, pinned to the inside of her coat gave the illusion of her latest dress. She took my place in front of the easel, told me not to move, and calmly began to draw my portrait. When the work was finished she had sucked and bitten all my pencils and lost my small eraser, and delighted, danced, sung and yelled, and walked all over a box of camembert. She demanded money from me for posing and left triumphantly, carrying her drawing with her. Three minutes later at the Café du Dôme a rich American collector bought this drawing for an outrageous price.

That day I wasn't sure which of the two of us was the painter.

The next morning, happily, it was I who was the painter. I made a large painting, *Nu couché de Kiki*. Autumn arrived, I sent it to the Salon d'Automne; it was the first time I had shown such a large painting.

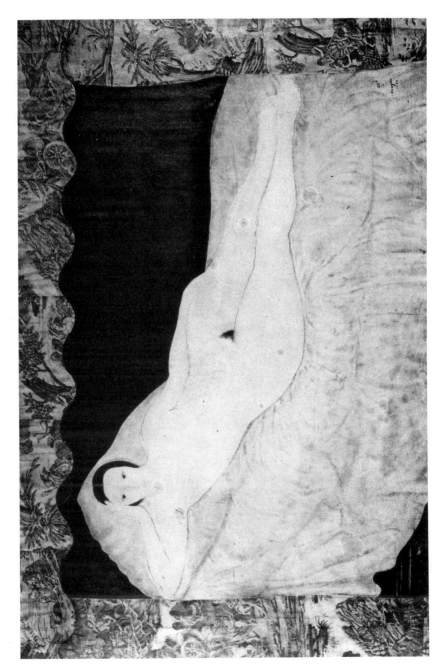

TSUGUHARU FOUJITA, *NU COUCHÉ À LA TOILE DE JOUY*, 1922

In the morning all the newspapers talked about it.

At noon the Minister congratulated me.

In the evening, for the sum of 8,000 francs, it was sold to a famous collector. The buyer for the State arrived too late. It was an immense success.

Kiki and I were each equally pleased; for the second time I wasn't sure who was the artist.

When I held the bundle of large bills tightly in my hand, I was worried; I didn't feel I had earned them, but had stolen them, because at that time my art dealer paid me only seven francs fifty centimes for each painting.

What joy! What a celebration! What a high! Without hesitating, I whispered into Kiki's ear, "Close your beautiful eyes," and one by one, I slipped several beautiful bills into her hand. Kiki went crazy and gasped open-mouthed.

Not losing a second, she ran out and disappeared like a cannon ball toward rue de la Gaîté.

An hour later I received a visit from a pretty woman wearing a hat covered with flowers, a coat, and dress more beautiful than any on the covers of the fashion magazines, sporting shoes brilliantly shining like a mirror and carrying in her hand a bag overflowing with a huge amount of cosmetics, not to mention a perfume sample given her by the friendly merchant. It was Kiki, little Kiki. She had surprised me and made all her friends in the quarter mad with jealousy.

Montparnasse has changed. Kiki does not change.

It was only two days ago she said to me, "My big lover, when are you going to bring me the cloth you promised me, I have nothing to wear. If it is one meter wide, I need four meters, but if it is one meter 30 wide, three meters will do me. You will be a real sweetie, and I will love you for life."

AT A MONTPARNASSE RESTAURANT

INTRODUCTION

by

Ernest Hemingway

There are enough photographs of Kiki in this book so you can have some idea how she looked in the ten years that are just over. This is being written in nineteen hundred and twenty-nine and Kiki now looks like a monument to herself and to the era of Montparnasse that was definitely marked as closed when she, Kiki, published this book.

Decades end every ten years dating from any original occurrence, such as the birth of Christ, or the end of the war, but eras can end any time. No one knows when they begin, at least not at the time, and the ones that are noted and advertised at the start usually do not stand up very long; the Era that was to start with Locarno, for instance.

An Era is easy to start in the newspapers; editorial writers start them regularly, but people forget all about them and they have nothing to do with real Eras. I hope no one will be rude enough at this point to consult a dictionary and find out what an Era really and exactly is because that might spoil all this big writing. The essential in big writing is to use words like the West, the East, Civilization, etc., and very often these words do not mean a damned thing but you cannot have big writing without them. My own experience has been that when you stand with your nose toward the north, if your head is held still, what is on your right will be east and what is on your left will be west and you can write very big putting those words in capitals but it is very liable not to mean anything.

However to get back to Eras, which is another big way of writing, although nobody knows when they start everybody is pretty sure when they are over and when, in one year, Kiki became monumental and Montpar-

nasse became rich, prosperous,brightly lighted, dancing-
ed, shredded-wheated, grape-nuts-ed or grapenutted
(take your choice, gentlemen, we have all these break-
fast foods now) and they sold caviar at the Dome, well,
the Era for what it was worth, and personally I don't
think it was worth much, was over.

Montparnasse for this purpose means the cafés and
the restaurants where people are seen in public. It
does not mean the apartments, studios and hotel rooms
where they work in private. In the old days the difference between the workers and those that didn't work
was that the bums could be seen at the cafés in the
forenoon. This of course was not entirely true as the
greatest bums, using the word in the American rather
than in the English connotation, did not rise until about
five o'clock when, on entering the cafés, they would
drink in friendly competition with the workers who had
just knocked off work for the day. The worker goes
to the café with the lonesomeness that a writer or
painter has after he has worked all day and does not
want to think about it until the next day but instead

see people and talk about anything that is not serious and drink a little before supper. And maybe during and after supper, too, depending on the individual. It was also very pleasant, after working, to see Kiki. She was very wonderful to look at. Having a fine face to start with she had made of it a work of art. She had a wonderfully beautiful body and a fine voice, talking voice, not singing voice, and she certainly dominated that era of Montparnasse more than Queen Victoria ever dominated the Victorian era.

The Era is over. It passed along with the kidneys of the workers who drank too long with the bums. The bums were fine people and proved to have the stronger kidneys finally. But then they rested during the day. Still that Era is over.

Kiki still has the voice. We do not have to worry about her kidneys, she comes from Burgundy where they make these things better than they do in Illinois or Massachusetts, and her face is as fine a work of art as ever. It is just that she has more material to work with now ; but you have the photographs in the book

THE FAMOUS POSTCARD OF KIKI AS QUEEN OF MONTPARNASSE

and then you have the book.   The book is supposed to be the point of this.

The people who tell me which books are great lasting works of art are all out of town so I cannot make an intelligent judgment, but I think Kiki's book is with the best I have read since The Enormous Room.   Maybe it won't translate, but if it does not seem any good to you, learn French and read it.   It won't hurt to learn to read French anyway and by then you will have forgotten all about this.   But in case you do learn it, it was Kiki's book I said to read, not Julian Green's (*) nor Jean Cocteau's, nor whoever should be at that time great French writers for Americans.   Read it all, from start to finish, the last chapter does not matter and does it no good, but you will not mind it after you have read Chapter VII called Initiation Manquée or Ma Grand'-mère which is Chapter XII.

———————

(*)   I have never read Mr. Green so this reference is probably very unjust. They tell me he is very good.   So let me withdraw the advice, or rather change it to urge you after having learned French, to read *both* Kiki and Mr. Green.

This is the only book I have ever written an introduction for and, God help me, the only one I ever will. It is a crime to translate it.   If it shouldn't be any good in English, and reading it just now again and seeing how it goes, I know it is going to be a bad job for whoever translates it, please read it in the original.   It is written by a woman who, as far as I know, never had a Room of Her Own, but I think a part of it will remind you, and some of it will bear comparison with, another book with a woman's name written by Daniel Defoe.   If you ever tire of books written by present day lady writers of all sexes, you have a book here written by a woman who was never a lady at any time.   For about ten years she was about as close as people get nowadays to being a Queen but that, of course, is very different from being a lady.

MOISE KISLING, *TORSO OF KIKI*, 1927

A NOTE ON KIKI,

ST. THERESA AND THE VULGATE

by the Translator

It was not until I had, temerariously, agreed to undertake the translation of Kiki's *Memoirs* that I was shown the Introduction which Mr. Ernest Hemingway had written for those same *Memoirs*. That Introduction was enough to frighten off a hardier hand than mine ; but I had given my word ; I was in for it.

As a matter of fact, I had my doubts before reading Mr. Hemingway on the subject. I may add that I have them still. I still do not know whether or not it is possible to translate Kiki.

Every translation, of course, is an impossibility ; it is only when the impossible has been achieved that the translator has done a day's work and is entitled to sit down to his *vin blanc*, his *frites* and his *saucisson*. All translation is a miracle, but the miracle has been known to flower.

Personally, I do not flatter myself that I am a miracle-worker, but I do like to dabble in miracles. If fervor counts for anything, fervor and those mosaics with which the floor of hell is commonly reported to be inlaid, I may state that I have brought to my present task something, I believe, of the spirit that St. Jerome, patron saint of all translators, brought to the rendering of the Scriptures. Filled with a sense of my high calling, I have approached my task reverently, never once doubting the plenary inspiration of the text before me. At the same time, I have been true as always to the maxim of my great predecessor : *"Non verbum e verbo, sed sensum exprimere de sensu."*

Anyone who undertook to render the divine Kiki in any other manner, would be doomed to failure. Do not be deceived by her *naïvetés* or even her *gaucheries ;* her prose is the most subtle that I know. At rare

PER KROHG, *KIKI*, 1928

moments, you think of a remote sort of Anita Loos flapper ; but the next moment, you banish the thought as sacrilege. I know, absolutely, of no other prose with which to compare this ; I know of none so hiddenly delicate, so deceptively nuanced,—not even *Fanny Hill*. Can you imagine, for example, an American Kiki, if an American Kiki were conceivable, turning out such a document as this ? Greenwich Village never produced anything like Kiki or Kiki's several-sided art, and Montparnasse, in her, verily is justified of its fruits.

Something, it is true, is due to the French, with its emphasis of restraint. An English-speaking near-Kiki type, in New York or London, would become practically unintelligible to the general in the breadth and bawdiness of her argot. Slang, with us, tends to run a sliding scale, becoming with the professional tramp and the criminal a psychopathic-to-paranoiac manifestation. Something of the same thing may be true on certain Gallic levels ; but with a girl of Kiki's sort, slang is, rather, an adornment and, like all good ornament,

MAN RAY PAINTED KIKI IN 1924,
USING MUTED SHADES OF BROWN AND GRAY

depends for its effectiveness upon its spacing ; Kiki, I feel sure, uses far better language on the whole than does either her American or her British correspondent. In fact, Kiki's prose is as fine an example as any I know of that quality on which French classicists so pride themselves : *clarté*. And *clarté*, the French themselves will be the first to tell you, is a highly deceptive entity.

In translating Kiki, then, one has to be constantly on his guard not to betray her by too broad a stroke. On the other hand, there is that betrayal for the English reader which would consist in being always and too faithful to the French, however clear a reflection it may be of the author.   The problem is not to translate Kiki's text, but to translate Kiki.

To be able to do this, one must have the *feel* of Kiki, the feel of the café du Dome at five o'clock on a rainy, bleary, alcoholic morning. Yet, this is not enough ; it does not give the picture ; it is unfair to Kiki. What is needed is the feel of a St. Theresa who should suddenly materialize in the café du Dome at the hour mentioned. For Kiki is more like St. Theresa than any one I know. That is why I am proud to be her St. Jerome. May God and Kiki forgive me, and then, perhaps, Mr. Hemingway will !

S. P.

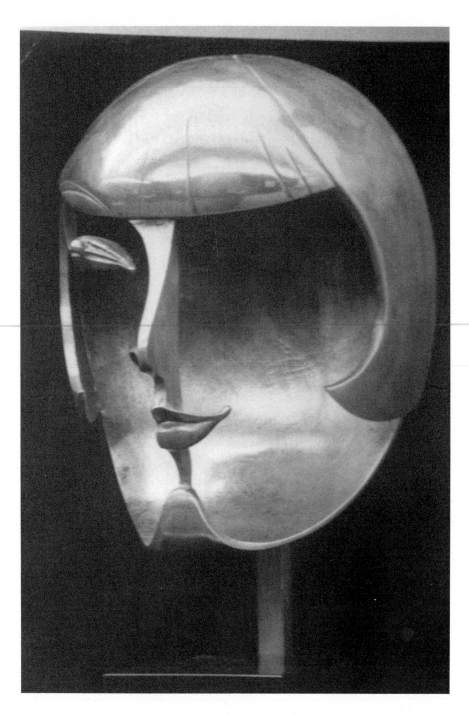

PABLO GAGALLO'S HEAD OF KIKI

PUBLISHER'S NOTE : *Kiki's Memoirs set all Paris in a turmoil when they appeared last year in the original French version. The Paris press was in a hubbub about them. The journals of the extreme right as those of the extreme left, and the intermediate ones, devoted columns of space to Kiki and her book.*

I could not without affectation show myself indifferent to the success which the Memoirs had met with. It was from me that Kiki received the first suggestion to write them. For over two years I continued urging her to buckle down to the job. Generous enough with promises, she always stopped short of performance, until a better man made his appearance at court,—the enterprising, persuasive Henri Broca, who understood how to make Kiki alive to the gravity of promises and take pen in hand.

She finally wrote the enrapturing, rough and ready chapters which make up the Memoirs, and Broca published the French edition. The issue of the English version devolved on me, and Kiki amplified it by the addition of about twenty pages of manuscript which are absent from the French edition.

Now Ernest Hemingway and Samuel Putnam have in some subtle sort of impersonal manner managed to get at loggerheads over the English translation. I have a good mind joining in the fray myself and taking up the cudgels, but only to hit both on the head.

Hemingway wrote the introduction with great gusto, unburdened himself of some comment on the difficulties, or impossibility of the translation,—in the abstract, of course, since he had not seen Putnam's,—packed his gear and tackle, and went off to Cuba on a fishing trip. And yet Hemingway possesses to perfection, in English, the very idiom which Kiki wields so matchlessly in French.

Putnam went Hemingway one better. He started out by saying that the translation of the Memoirs was impos-

sible, and, then, coming down to solid earth, delivered it to me—a capital job—for publication. Both these gentlemen were simply decanting poppycock. One is tempted to retort in the pertinent invective of the Scriptures (Acts, II, 13), which so blithely disposes of a similar controversy concerning language : "These are full of new wine."

So long as human nature continues one and universal, any language reducible from it must of necessity be translatable into another. Putnam is merely kidding when he rates every translation among miracles. His own so-called patron saint, Jerome, whom he quotes, did not consider translation a miracle, or, if he did, acted in a most low-brow and profane manner about it, when, realizing his weakness in Hebrew, the language he had undertaken to translate from, he hired himself a walking vocabulary and grammar in the person of a 100 % hebraistically efficient old Jew, from whom he learned with great avidity, and then produced the immortal Vulgate. It appears the Jew instructed Jerome only at night, having had some other occupation in the day time. The venerable professor's apposite day job was probably that of candle maker.

Thus we stumble upon the early origins of night schools.

No, there is no miracle inherent in translation. To call knowledge of languages a miracle is an empty boast and a useless boost. Language may be jugglery. And difficult. Two languages, double jugglery, and doubly difficult. An American bootlegger will find it easier to repeat the miracle of Cana than an American college to produce a graduate equipped with two languages and sufficient skill for their workmanlike employment. I would be the last to decry or undervalue the labor of translators. Their difficulties are not lightly brushed aside. Sometimes circumstances are particularly untoward. Annoying questions of taste frequently rise up to trouble translators profoundly. Again and again the memory cells need special prodding before they will consent to fall into gaps uncomfortably waiting to be stopped. But when all is said, these difficulties, with corresponding variations, are incidental alike to many crafts and occupations that demand skill. It is all in a day's work.

But, kidding or not, Putnam is in a bit of a mess.

ALEXANDER CALDER, *KIKI'S NOSE*, 1931

Even the Bible is agin him.   And that is serious for a man who leans on the Bible.   He has read his Saint-Jerome.   For queer outlandish reading commend me to Putnam.   But has he read Jerome's Vulgate ?

In the Revised Version, I Corinthians, XII, and surely in the Vulgate as well, there are listed a considerable number of spiritual gifts,—one definite gift to every man. So there is one man endowed with the power to work miracles ; *another has the gift of* tongues, *meaning that in addition to yiddish, or whatever else may be his mother tongue, he can bellyache equally well in some other language or languages ; while still another is gifted with the* inter-pretation of tongues.   *This last is rather a tricky way of putting it, for it may or may not foreshadow the Freu-dian achievement of translating the unconscious into the conscious.   It might also stand for expounders or commen-tators of the James Joyces of that interesting period.   Or it might simply mean putting into Greek or Latin or Assyrian what the American humanists might express so much more lucidly in Hebrew, or* vice versa.   *It may mean any of these or a host of other things.   But one thing*

Scriptural authority does *make clear is this,—that the miracle men were one distinct group, and the verbiage artists a guild apart, and that the members of the one never passed the time of day with the members of the other when they were out taking the air of a Sabbath afternoon.*

Yes, Saint Jerome translated the Bible under great difficulties. Insuperable we should be inclined to call them today. He had no one to take his dictation down in shorthand. No one to do his typing for him. Honest workman, in love with his job and its manifold difficulties, he never prated of miracles and impossibilities in connection with his monumental translations, and I fear he would have disapproved strongly of Putnam's doing so. On the other hand, having himself had a sister who had gone wrong and whom he had succeeded in leading back to a state of grace, it is a safe bet Saint Jerome would have liked Kiki's Memoirs, although he might not have found it easy to understand, how such of Kiki's favorites as Jean Cocteau could have the remotest share in a woman's ruin. He would have liked particularly the homespun colloquialism of Putnam's English version of the Memoirs and would have made no bones about saying so,—well protected as he would be by the great distance of time and space against a possible menace of Ernest Hemingway's gladiatorial hulk and sinewy arm.

(E. W. T.)

Photo Man Ray

Photo Mécano

AT AN ARTIST'S BALL, MAY 1929, HENRI BROCA STANDS BEHIND KIKI

Kiki's

MEMOIRS

KIKI, *CLASSROOM*, 1929

I

MY CHILDHOOD IN BURGUNDY

I was born October 2, 1901, in Burgundy.

My mother traipsed off to Paris, leaving me with my grandmother, who now found herself with half a dozen youngsters on her hands—her three daughters had made her a present of the job of bringing them up. . . . We were six little love-babies, our *fathers* having overlooked the little matter of *acknowledging* us, and my mother sent five francs a month to pay for my board.

My grandfather was a road-hand and earned a franc and a half a day. My grandmother went out by the day to wash or sew for the well-to-do folks in the neighbourhood. We were very poor, but we always had a nice mess of kidney-beans to eat.

When I was five or six years old, they put me in the

day-nursery. I remember, they gave me soup with bread in it to eat there. In the yard, there was a big bench, very long and very low, and I used to hike up my dress and sit down on it. I had a little playmate who was eight. His name was Henri, and he had long dark hair that fell down over his shoulders. I thought he was simply grand, because my own head was always peeled like a boy's.

This saved my grandmother a lot of work. My five cousins, both the boys and the girls, were peeled like me, and they used to run a scrub-brush over our heads to get the cooties out (which didn't keep me from having plenty of 'em just the same).

I didn't attend school very regularly, because the teacher was awful mean : she didn't care much about us poor kids ! She used to put us at the bottom of the class and punish us for nothing at all. She treated us as if we were lousy, and I didn't like that, even supposing that it was the truth. The worst punishment she could find for me was to stand me in a corner with my nose to the wall, and I used to stand for whole days like that.

LITTLE ALICE AND HENRI

I thought I'd die, I used to get so tired, and besides, it was a green wall, and that hurt my eyes.

Since we were very poor, we went twice a week to the Good Sisters to get some rice or kidney-bean-soup. This was some punishment for me and my girl-cousin, for the Sisters didn't like us.

We were dirty and not very religious, and so, every time I stuck my platter out, I could see a pair of hard, wicked eyes looking me over ; and then, I was sure to be scolded : "There you are again, you Prin young one ! What's the matter ? Can't your mother in Paris find enough for you to eat ? They say, there's money to be made in Paris . . . " And all the other kids' eyes and ears would pop, they'd be so surprised.

Oh ! they had to stand for plenty of it themselves, since we were all in the same boat. For my mother wasn't exactly rolling in wealth. She had got a job at Baudelocque as a nurse, and my board-money was always five francs a month.

But in the country, you can raise money out of anything ! We used to wait impatiently for the big

SISTER CORNETTE HANDS OUT FOOD

summer storms, so that we could go out in the beating rain and look for snails in the bushes and in the holes in the walls ; and then, there were also dandelions, which, when well washed and cleaned, could be sold for two sous the bowlful. . . We would go to look for strawberries in the woods and for mushrooms. All these little things helped keep the wolf away from the door. We also sold the things we stole, for we used to go prowling around in the fields and gardens. What else is a poor peasant to do ? Next door to my grandmother's was a fine house with a fine barn full of wood and coal. It was there, it seems, that my father lived. He had a wife and daughter, and was very good to them ; they had fine clothes to wear. My father never spoke to me, but he used to give me a funny look. I used to think he was especially grand when country-fair time came around and he was the orchestra-leader and athletic director. He was a big chap and handsome, so I've heard folks say. He had been obliged to leave my mother, after living with her for six years, in order to marry a woman who had a thousand francs and a pig.

II

MY ARRIVAL IN PARIS

I am twelve.

My mother writes to my grandmother to send me to Paris, so that I can learn to read. I am all cut up about it. It scares me to think I'm not going to see those schoolroom-seats any more . . . Besides, I'm crazy about my grandmother. After all, I hadn't seen very much of my mother. For me, she was a lady from Paris who came down every year to spend a month's vacation, and who brought me playthings, shiny shoes or a pretty dress.

My grandmother takes the train with me as far as Troyes, and there, she turns me over to the station-master, who sticks me into the first-class. He asks some lady to keep an eye on me, but all she gives me is a stony stare.

I must be a pretty-looking sight. I have very black, straggly hair and a blue beret that is too small for me, with a red topknot on it. My face is yellow, and I am skinny, and over my shoulders I've strapped a canvas-bag with my name sewed on it in red thread. I'm afraid they'll lose me !

Then, the train starts, and I begin to weep all over the place, and the lady keeps on looking at me all the time ! She asks me why I'm crying, and the only word I can say is : "Grandmother". I see she doesn't like me to cry ; and so, just to show how brave and strong I can be, I take a big hunk of sausage with garlic in it and a little bottle of red wine out of my canvas-bag.

I eat, I drink, I cry. My sausage is stinking up the whole car, and the lady appears to be absolutely disgusted !

I keep on crying.

The train gets to Paris, and they turn me over to my mother, who was nearly scared to death, she was

BOUND FOR PARIS

so afraid I was lost. But the truth is, if you want to know, I had a figure that you'd have a hard time passing up anywhere.

They put me into a horse-cab. My mother goes off into convulsions when I ask her if they go over the nice shiny Paris streets with wax, because that must mean a lot of work for somebody.

III

MY FIRST JOBS

I am thirteen past.

I have just quit school for good. I know how to read and count—that's all !

I get a job as a knitter's apprentice, and I work there for a while. One of my mother's girl-friends tells her that I can earn three francs a day in a factory, where they repair soldiers' shoes.

The war is on.

The shoes come in from the front to be disinfected, and they send them back to the factory to be dipped in oil so as to soften up the leather. My job is to put them on wooden trees so they can be hammered into shape again. Afterwards, I had other jobs : soldering ; dirigible balloons ; aeroplanes ; grenades.

My mother and I had barely enough to make both ends meet. At noon, I ate in a cheap hash-joint for eight sous; but even at that, they left entirely too much gravel in the beans !

On Saturday, my mother and I go to some friends of ours who are flower-merchants in the rue Mouffetard. I like that a lot. In the morning, I go to Les Halles with Mother Guinoiseau and her youngsters, two girls of my age and five boys, and then, from ten to two, we sell flowers.

In the rue Mouffetard, next to me, I have a terrible rival who keeps bawling out louder than me : "Buy some garlic or shallot !" The older one of the girls who is selling with me is a big, handsome blonde. The really extraordinary thing about her is her hands, the hands of a queen. We try to see who can make up the most like a gypsy, that is, who can put the most oil on her hair to make her spit-curls stay put, and then, we stick in a lot of combs, with stones of all colors and

KIKI, *FIRST LOVE*, 1930

copper jewelry. In the afternoon, we go to the Flea Market, Porte d'Italie. That is where you get fitted out : shoes for a bargain at one franc fifty or two francs ; petticoats and underwear for five or ten francs ; and then, at night, we have fried potatoes to eat with white wine. They give us free rein and let us go to the movies like big girls. We have our sweeties waiting for us there. Mine is named Dédé ; he is a big blond fellow with a surly mug, and is about nineteen years old. He makes some hit with me because he's staying with a woman. She's the one who does the work, I guess ; he doesn't do anything. I'm in love with him. At the movies, he never leaves my mouth alone, and on Monday, I go back to the grind and wait impatiently for the next Saturday to come around. My mother had noticed that I had a big mark the color of eggplant on my neck. I spit on my handkerchief, but it wouldn't go away. I was wondering what it could be, when I got such a box on the ear that it knocked me silly . . . I hadn't thought that kisses left marks, too ; I'll know better after this.

Such luck ! I have just found out that my good looking Dédé is a little thief, and that he had been pinched one night when he was burglarizing a shoe store in the avenue des Gobelins. He hasn't gone down any in my estimation ; quite the contrary ; I, who have been reading *Fantomas*, always think of him as one of the heroes out of my books. I do so like to read, but that doesn't keep me from being a wall-flower. I have a horror of stockings ; I have a passion for yellow socks. . .

My mother has some artificial red geraniums on the mantelpiece ; I swipe a petal every day to rouge my cheeks and mouth.

And then, I sew up my corset with string ; it is so much more substantial !

The only trouble is, there are some folks who go around sticking their noses in everywhere they have no business to be, and some of these up and told my mother that I looked like a tart, I was so painted up. (As if you *could* look like that at thirteen !)

When my mother wants to tease me, she stuffs cotton into my corsets to make it look as if I have a pair of big breasts, and then she struts up and down in front of the door, and if one of my sweeties happens to pass, she says to him : "Look at Alice, will you, the big flirt ! . . ." But that doesn't bother me. I have so many sweeties !

To get the Guinoiseau family over with, they buried the grandmother in the cemetery at Bagneux. Since they had to bring the two little brats along, they seated them on the steps of the hearse. When it was all over, the family hurried off as usual to drown their sorrow in white wine, fried potatoes and sausages. But the end of the party was not nearly so funny. Everybody was drunk : punches in the jaw, fights, fights ; black crêpe hats rolled in the gutter, the brats bawled, and everybody was saying "sh—". When the fight was over, they all made up with more white wine, more fried potatoes and more sausages.

The war is on. My mother earns barely enough money to keep herself. As for me, the ten sous a week I earn do not go very far.

I have an aunt and some cousins at Troyes ; my

COURTYARD OF HOTEL L'AIGLON, 1926

mother sends me down to them, because there I can earn three francs a day in a spinning mill.

I reached Troyes at the beginning of winter ; my aunt lives on the outskirts of the town. I am very well satisfied. My aunt reminds me somehow of a big overgrown policeman. She is not what you might call mean, but she is all the time bawling herself hoarse, and she has a certain smell about her that I never did like. She always has her snuff-box in her hand.

And there is cousin Eugénie, gotten up fit to kill ; she's the one who wears the breeches in that house. She had a lover two years before the war, and had a child by him. He never came back . . . Probably killed in the war.

My aunt worships her grandson. There is also Madeleine, her other daughter, who is thirteen ; she's a redhead ; a flaming red is what I mean, and she's the laughing stock of the family.

There are but two small rooms. My aunt sleeps with Eugénie, the kid between them, and I sleep with the redhead.

We set out every morning, the three of us, for the mill. We come back at noon, as fast as we can ! to drink what is supposed to be coffee, with no sugar in it, and to make a feast on herring, for they only cost two sous apiece. In the evening, the redhead goes to get us something at the canteen next door. It is better than the red herrings we had at noon, but the poor redhead is not allowed to sit down at table ; she has only bread crusts to eat . . . "She eats less of it," says my aunt. She gets only the coffee grounds, and she has to take care of the kid, who is cross and filthy. He talks enough to be able to tell my aunt amazing stories, and my aunt then jumps on the redhead and sends her to bed without her supper.

I am young, myself, and find it hard to understand exactly the position this poor redhead is in, but every time I sit down at table I get a catch in my throat when I look over and see her sitting there under the window, on a wooden stool, eating her supper out of her lap. It is often enough that she goes to bed without any supper, but I generally manage to sneak some dry bread for her, and sometimes a little something else to go along with it. Poor redhead ! I can remember her pale white skin and her thin little bosom ; my grandmother had brought us all up until we reached the age of twelve, and so, she was just like a sister to me.

I stayed there only three months, on account of an accident that happened to my foot.

Well, here I am back at Paris, where I have told my mother everything, especially about the poor redhead. The redhead stayed on down there in the country, where she married a wood cutter and has a baby, but she still feels very bitterly toward her mother, and her health is very bad.

ON A RARE TRIP TO MONTMARTRE

IV

MAID-OF-ALL-WORK

I am fourteen and a half, and my mother has just got me a job with a baker-lady in the place Saint-Charles. Board, laundry and thirty francs a month.

In the morning, up at five, to serve one or two sous' worth of bread to the men on their way to work. At seven, deliver the bread to the house-customers and climb up and down all those flights of stairs—that made me out of breath, I'll tell you! Back at nine to straighten up the house, run errands and spend a quarter of an hour in a big flour-closet. My job is to keep a big iron bar going so as to let the flour down into the strainer. I come out white as a mouse. Then, I have to help the baker take the bread out of the oven. This baker used to strip naked and make dirty jokes for my benefit. "Look, Alice, look ! You'll never see another one like that !"

Back to the kitchen !

The missus is a mean old dried-up thing. She can't give an order without yelling her head off. At night, I can only think of one thing : I can't get to bed quick enough, I'm so darned tired.

I'd like to make a getaway. But where can I go, without any money ? And besides, if I did that, my mother would stick me in reform-school till I'm twenty-one.

I remember, I had an eighteen-year-old aunt who died from the way they treated her there. In the middle of winter, they fastened her head under a cold-water-faucet and let the water run down over her neck until she was ready to do what they wanted her to. Her name was Alice, she was bull-headed, and since it seemed that, so far as anybody could make out, I had her temper, they gave me the same name.

And anyway, I've made up my mind to wait until something happens and gives me a good excuse to quit.

One morning, when the weather is very swell, I open my window and look down into the square. I see there, upon a bench, a little nursemaid who is letting somebody kiss her.

I had such a funny feeling! I rolled over in my bed, and it was awful nice. . . and after that, I was afraid.

Two or three times that day, I simply had to go off by myself and be alone . . .

Photo Man Ray

KIKI DANCING IN THE WHITE DRESS

V

LOVE WAKES

I've noticed a lad who lives in the square, right across the way from my room. He is short and dumpy with a wicked look. I am thinking about taking him into the back room some evening and letting him make me.

He's kissed me and loved me up, but I haven't quite got the nerve !

Nothing happens at all, and I go back upstairs to my room, promising him that there'll be something doing some of these days.

VI

FIRST CONTACT WITH ART

The missus has gone a little bit too far !

She treated me as if I was a greenhorn, just because I blackened my eyebrows with burnt matches.

I jumped on her and gave her a good beating, and she didn't even try to keep me off.   The baker separated us, and whispered to me, "That's the stuff !   You ought to have killed her !"

I've packed up my things.

She won't give me my month's pay ; so there's nothing for me to do but to beat it ; but since it's eight o'clock at night, I don't know just where to go.   Then, I remember a woman from my part of the country that I met a few days before and whose address I have.

The next day, I went out to look for work, and I met an old sculptor who, seeing that I was up against it, had me come and pose for him. That was something new for me, to strip like that, but what else was there to do ! I've already posed for him three sittings. But since his studio is not very far from my mother's place, folks have told her that her daughter was undressing in men's rooms.

My mother forced her way into the sculptor's and proceeded to throw a scene. I was posing, and she began to scream that I wasn't her daughter any more, that I was nothing but a dirty wh—.

That didn't mean anything to me !

It even cheered me up a little, because I understood now that the game was up.

A SECOND POSE WEARING THE WHITE DRESS WITH LACE

VII

AN INITIATION THAT FAILED TO COME OFF

I've looked up the woman from down my way.

I've been living with her since yesterday in a dark little room in the Plaisance quarter. She's told me that she's being kept by a working-man, an old Corsican who's not so young any more. He gives her two francs a day and supplies her with sausage and cheese which he gets from home. I've been in the same room with them when they went to bed and made love. I watched them and didn't think anything about it ; it was a good chance to fill up on sausage. A day or two later, my girl-friend took me for a walk with her down the boulevards. We had been at the concert Mayol for a try-out in the nude, and they'd told us to come back in a few hours and they'd see about hiring us. We were in the boulevard Strasbourg ; it was stinging cold, and a light snow was falling all the time.

My friend suggested my letting myself... be seduced by an old man, saying there was nothing like it, when it came to losing your virginity painlessly. That scared me plenty, but I thought what she said was true enough.

As we walked along we saw a man of fifty coming toward us. He was pale and close-shaved—not bad at all ! He made quite a hit with me, especially when my girl friend told me he must surely be an actor.

He smiled at us and offered to buy us a cup of coffee and some rolls. And then it was, my friend told him that he would have to initiate me, that I was perfectly willing, and that he would be doing me a great favor !

I stayed behind with him, and we went to Ménilmontant where he lived. His apartment was on the fifth floor and struck me as being the ritz. He made me take off my clothes and gave me one of his big nightgowns.

We had had dinner : some nice roast pork with potatoes and some good wine.

I learned that he did a clown act with his wife, who was on tour at the time. He had any number of pretty costumes, all glittering with sparkling stones, like those the Fratellinis wear. I stood there with my mouth open, while he picked up a guitar and sang a little song. I was a little gone on him already. That song, I'll never forget it !

It went like this ! (For two voices).

The moon is shining high,
She's listening in tonight
On a little lullaby,
So hopeful and so bright.
And you can hear her say :
"Lovers, hurry, do !"
Then smiling goes her way,
Up in the sky so blue.

He made me get ready for bed, and I lay down very

happy at the thought that I was going to learn all about love at last.

For I liked this man, he was so gentle and such a tease !

He lay down beside me and did ever so many nice things.

But in the morning, when I left, I was still a virgin, alas !

VIII

ROBERT

I had stopped in Montparnasse, in front of a Chinese art-store. My girl-friend, who had a date, had left me... The snow had pasted down my hair and taken all the curl out, and I was hungry as a wolf.

All of a sudden, I felt some one behind me, for it was almost night. Already, the fellow was speaking to me. He was tall and skinny, with a pair of sharp little eyes.

He came up to me and said : "You'll get lost, if you don't watch out, Mademoiselle." And then, he offered to take me to his studio for a cup of chocolate. I weakened when I heard that word, chocolate, and studio made me think of an artist ; and so, I took him up !

After we'd had some chocolate, steaming hot, and my tummy was full, I didn't care whether I left or not. Besides, I always was curious, and I wanted to find out about love some time or other !

As we climbed the stairs up into the loft, I was shaking all over. I was very much afraid of this man, for I didn't have as much confidence in him as I'd had in the other . . . He had a wicked face, and he kept sticking it up into mine . . .

He didn't have any toes in his socks ; they were like mittens. He told me that was the fashion, and it was perfectly all right with me. Anyway, I wanted him to make me.

. . . .

I screamed and suffered. He was very awkward, and although he wasn't able to give me what I wanted, I loved him all the more, for the reason that I had hopes. At the end of a month's time, I was still a half-virgin. As for Robert, he used to bring in women from the Dôme and have affairs with them in front of me !

I had a wretched time of it. He insisted that I should go out in the boulevard ; there were a lot of handsome American soldiers there, he told me. He beat me and bawled me out, because "I wasn't good for anything" ! I kept looking for work but wasn't able to find any.

One day, I found myself in the boulevard Sebastopol, tired to death and absolutely all-in. A negro looked at me. He scared me . . . he was so black. . . I was crying so I couldn't see, I was so discouraged. . . .Then, some woman who was doing the pave touched me on the shoulder and said : "Hard luck, huh ! poor kid ? I haven't any sous, but here are four stamps ; go and see if you can sell them !" Women like that are too grand for words. They've got a heart.

I had some hard times after that. One day, I got a job posing in the rue Saint-Jacques. It was at a painter's, and he gave me some tea. He didn't have the money to pay me, and what's more, he tried to make me.

I knew that my lover was waiting for me to bring

KIKI IN MAN RAY'S ROOM AT THE HOTEL DES ÉCOLES

him some money to eat on. When I got to the Gare Montparnasse, I sat down on a bench and tried to keep from crying. On the same bench, at the other end, was a very old man with a nice little package of some sort. I thought it must be cakes, and so, I kept looking his way. He looked at me, and I up and told him what had happened. He said : "Come around behind the station and show me your breasts, and I'll give you three francs."

I was so afraid of going home without any money that, in spite of the fact that I couldn't stand him, I did what he wanted me to, and I had my three francs.

I went home, happy as a lark, with some bread and cheese. I had already forgotten all about my troubles, with him . . .

And then, one day, he put me out, telling me that he was leaving for Brittany with a friend of his.

IX

RUE DE VAUGIRARD

Robert's friend lent me his studio, and the same day, I got acquainted with a charming danseuse, who gave me something to eat, dressed me out from head to foot, and made me bob my hair à la Ninon.

After that, I met a painter who, besides his painting, was interested in aeroplanes. He gave me a job as helper, and I was tickled to death. He even gave me twenty francs on account.

Then, the danseuse went away on tour, and I went to live in the rue de Vaugirard, in an old house with a long hall. After this hall, you crossed a little square court and went down a dozen steps or so, where the cellars were and a couple of tiny rooms with casement-windows. I didn't care much about this new place. It had a moldy smell, like mushrooms. There was a woman next door to me that I almost never saw ; she did the pave from the corner of the rue de Vaugirard and the boulevard Montparnasse. We used to nod to each other when we met ; and every Sunday, her lover would come to stay all night with her.

One day, I had some scare, I'll tell you ! when this woman next door got into an argument with some guy on the outside, at her door. She called out "Madame Kiki !" but I didn't answer. She kept yelling that some one was trying to douse her with sulphuric acid, and for me to go get the concierge. Lucky for me, the concierge's husband had heard the noise and had just come up with a gun.

But those chaps had already left !

Me, too ; I lost no time in getting out of there.

X

AN UNUSUAL LODGING

I had got acquainted with a young fellow who lived at home, and he had told me that he would get me out of trouble any time that I found myself with no place to sleep. One of his uncles had a shed in behind the Gare Montparnasse where I could go in a case like that. And so, I went there and slept on a bag of sand. It was spring, and I would wrap up in his overcoat, which he would lend me the night before and come get in the morning. The lights from the station dazzled me, but I managed to sleep all right enough, and I wasn't the least bit afraid. In the morning, I would go wash up in my room in the rue de Vaugirard, where I didn't stay any more from fear of sulphuric acid scenes.

XI

MR. W . . .

In my down-and-out days, that is, in 1917, I knew a sculptor who sometimes put me up. One day, he said to me : "Kiki, I'm going to send you to take a piece of sculpture to a nutty guy, down in a swell quarter !" I went, and when I rang the bell, I thought it was a maid who was coming to the door, but it was the guy himself. I couldn't get a very good look at him, at first shot, because there weren't any windows in his place ; the only light he had was through some big panes, like the kind they have in churches, all colored, with lamps behind them. He was very nice and friendly-like, and right off the bat, he says to me : "Will you step

Photo Man Ray

1917

this way, little girl ? " I trailed after him, through a lot of rooms ; and in the kitchen, I caught sight of dishes and silverware spilled around all over the floor, covered with moss and greenish-colored rust and filled with mushrooms !

We crossed a big diningroom ; and lined up against the wall, there were all of fifty guns.

We then went into an enormous studio, expensively furnished. He showed me a collection of butterflies and some dresses that came from China with perfectly marvellous embroidery. He had me try one on. I slipped on some white silk stockings and then went back to the other end of the apartment.

I was in a smokingroom. He put me on a divan and then started some electric apparatus to going that was used for polishing elephants' bristles. He said it was for making bracelets.

Now and then, I could see him take a little box with a pretty little spoon in it and stick the spoon up his nose ! I didn't know what it was all about, until he went out and left me alone. I then did the same thing he had done, and I suddenly felt very happy. I forgot to tell you that the sculptor had warned me that everything here was scattered around all over the floor, and that it was not uncommon to find banknotes and jewelry there. But he also warned me not to take anything, for the gentleman had put in a system of mirrors, and he would be sure to see me.

So, I didn't take very much of a chance; I only stole five francs. I felt happy, rich . . . the cocaïne was getting in its work! Then, the gentleman said to me: "Come along; I'm going to take you out to dinner, in a very swell restaurant in the Champs-Elysées." And he lent me some rings and beautiful diamonds for the occasion. But I couldn't eat much of anything, for the coke had taken away all the appetite I had.

I stayed with him a day or two and then went back to Montparnasse.

When, a couple of days later, he telephoned me to come see him, I stuck him up. For I had other fish to fry.

And that was the last I ever heard of him!

XII

MY GRANDMOTHER

My grandmother was a good old soul; I don't think I've ever heard her say that such and such things were done and such and such things were not done : everything went with her.

When I went down to see her once or twice a year, I could take any one with me that I liked. When she saw me making up, a smile would come in her eyes, and she would say : "You're a pretty lass, Alice ! My, how nice you smell !" She liked for me to comb her hair, and I used to have fun doing it up in crazy ways. She liked, too, for me to clean out her wrinkles with eau de Cologne ; for she had so many wrinkles, and there were

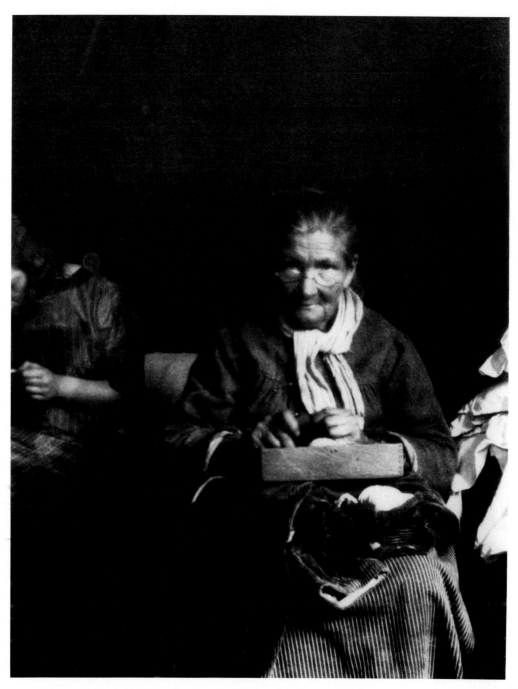

Photo Kiki

KIKI'S GRANDMOTHER AND HER COUSIN MADELEINE FAR LEFT

such gobs of dirt in them ! The only memories that mean anything to my grandmother are from the year 1870, when she slapped a Prussian for pinching her thighs. She'll tell you, also, that her husband gave her a crack once, when they were first married.

But her greatest adventure was during the last war, when many Americans were camping in the fields around Châtillon. For my grandmother, and it's the truth I'm telling you, is like me in one respect : she's very curious. I'm only surprised that her curiosity hasn't got her into more scrapes than it has ! One day, when she had been a long way from home and was coming back, she caught sight of a woman who was running away for dear life, and behind a tree, she saw a young American soldier making a bed of leaves on the ground. She came up close to find out what he was up to, when the American came over to her with some money in his hand. He finally made her understand that, in spite of her age, he'd like . . . My grandmother understood at last, and had such a scare that she forgot all about her cartload of wood and began running as hard as she could tear across a field of beets, which is not exactly an easy thing to do.

"That young brat", she would say, "wanted to rape me right there in the woods".

My grandmother had a friend who got a nice little house for herself by laying a leg often enough with young Americans. . . And the one big regret in my grandmother's life was not having a little house of her own. . .But what do you expect, she simply couldn't, that's all !

XIII

SOUTINE PERIOD

Here's how I came to know Soutine.

I was coming out of a show with a girl-friend who
was as much up against it as I was! Since we only had
a few francs in our pockets, not enough for a room, my
friend told me that she would take me to see a Russian
who lived in the cité Falguière. "You'll see. You'll
have some nice suet-cakes to eat, some tea to drink, and
it's nice and warm there." So, we went there, and were
climbing the little staircase when we heard voices . . .
He had a woman with him. We stood there, glued to
the stairs. It was so cold . . . We had been splashing
around in the melting snow. We stood there, on that

THE CHECKERED FLOOR DATES THIS PHOTO TO 1924

staircase, until two o'clock in the morning, frozen stiff but without the slightest idea where to go. Then, I began to cry. She told me that, maybe, it would be our luck to find Soutine at home ; he lived in the house next door. Just as we were going out, Soutine appeared. He was so fierce looking that I was a little bit afraid, but my girl-friend bucked me up. We went into a studio where it was only a little bit less cold than it was outside, but Soutine spent the night burning up everything in his place to keep us warm. Ever since that day, I've had a crush on Soutine ; we've been together steady for some time now.

He had a couple of friends who were also very nice to me. We made a fine quartet, us four ! At that period, I was trigged out in all the glad-rags of the Quarter : a man's hat ; an old cape ; three-toed shoes, you might say . . .

If it had been a little warmer, I'd have gone bare-foot, for I fell all over myself every step I took.

XIV

MY FIRST APPEARANCE

IN ARTISTIC CIRCLES

The Saint-Ouen factory where I had got a job decided to let out the young women and to keep only the old working-men's wives, those with children to support or with a husband at the front. Once more, I found myself out of work and without any money.

I often used to go by the Dôme or the Rotonde and look in to see if I could spot any artists. It took a lot of nerve for me to go and spend a couple of francs in dolling myself up on the chance of earning enough for coffee-and. But as luck would have it, I met there the same young chap who had lent me his overcoat to sleep in at night, and I also got acquainted with a bunch of his friends, but they were in as bad a fix as I was myself. Young painters that I went home with, to spend most of my nights in posing and singing. We had tea to drink. One of them had traveled a good deal and had some swell stories to tell. There was also a young blond chap that I took a liking to. We spent some time together, standing up at the Rotonde bar, but Libion didn't like my looks, because I didn't have any hat. He only let me stand at the bar ; he wouldn't let me go in the back room. How I envied those pretty women that I could see there, who seemed to be right at home ! Some one made me a present of a hat, and Libion perked up a little . . . He seemed to have got used to my mug !

I got acquainted with other fellows and did more and more posing. Posing is something I'm not very crazy about, for I've got a pilose system that's not as well developed as it might be in a certain spot, and so, I have to dab myself up with black chalk.

But I can give a swell imitation of hair !

XV

MONTPARNASSE LIFE

Little by little, I made my way into artistic circles, so full of wayward charm.

Since I didn't always have a room, I stayed sometimes with one and sometimes with another, most often with married couples. I was so very gay that my poverty didn't make even so much as a dent ; and such words as "kill-joy", "gloom", "the blues" were just so much Hebrew so far as I was concerned—they simply didn't register with me ! What's more, I didn't know what it was to be sick.

I used to go to Rosalie's to eat, in the rue Campagne-Première. There, I'd order soup. Sometimes, I'd get myself bawled out plenty for having the nerve not to spend more than six sous on a plate of soup. Other times, Rosalie would almost sob, and feed me for nothing.

The customer who got her goat the most of all was Modigliani. All he did was growl ; he used to make me shiver from head to foot.

But maybe he wasn't good-looking !

There was also Utrillo ; I don't remember much about him. I only know that once, after I had been posing for him, I went around to take a look and see what he had done and was knocked off my pins to discover that he had been drawing a little country house. There were some folks came in bringing some drawings which he had made on the corner of a table. They were anxious to get them signed by him, and they went off looking as happy as fools.

MAURICE MENDJIZKY'S PORTRAIT OF KIKI PAINTED AROUND 1918

XVI

1918

I'm keeping house with a painter.

It's not exactly what you would call high-life ; but anyway, we eat ! But I've got to go to work ; and so, I go to stand in line at the employment-agencies. I land a job with Potin. I get a hundred francs a month rinsing bottles.

But as luck would have it, I've got a wisdom-tooth coming, which puckers up my mouth so that I can't even get a teaspoon inside it. Since I can't eat, I can hardly go on putting my hands in water to rinse botles : that makes me all the hungrier !

I've found another job, in a book-bindery. After

eight hours work, I have a finger that's almost sawed in two. Then, I get a felon and have to stop work.

The first hundred years are the hardest !

From drinking too much tea and eating too much toast, my health was not all it might be at this time ; and one night, I went to bed and thought I surely was going to die. I was in such misery with my heart, and my friend was so frightened, that he picked up the scrub rag which they used on the floor, dipped it in water and began rubbing me with it. My sufferings kept up, and so, I slipped on a coat with not a stitch on underneath it and set out on foot for the Cochin Hospital.

When I got there, they made me take a bath and put on the regulation uniform. My heart kept hurting me all the time, and the young interne who was there gave me a terrified look and whispered something in my friend's ear. That didn't help put a stop to my palpitations. Then the nurse put me to bed and said to me : "There, you see what you get for not being a good girl !'' Those idiots thought I had been taking cocaine !

I stayed four days in the hospital. From time to time, I had a spell with my heart. The doctors said : ''It's a nervous case ; there's nothing to be done !''

I couldn't bear to stay there very long. I should have died of fright, especially in the evening when there was only one little lamp to light up that big room where all you could hear was moans and death-rattles . . .

The nurses were rude and insolent. I got into a mix-up with one of them for abusing a woman 101 years old who had wet the bed. The nurse had shouted into her ear : ''Aren't you ashamed of yourself, doing a thing like that at your age.'' Then, one night when this poor old woman tried to ask for the pot with a voice so weak that the nurse couldn't hear it, I put my hands up to my mouth like a megaphone and yelled : ''The pot, if you please !''

The nurse was peeved about it. I told her that, so far as I was concerned, I had come there to die, and that since I didn't seem to be able to, I was going to leave the next morning. I spoke to the doctor and left. I just wonder if it wouldn't be a lot better for women like that, with no more patience than they have, to go out and get jobs as street cleaners.

XVII

1920

I leave the house this morning very early.

I go to the Rotonde or the Parnasse Bar, where there's an Arab who comes every morning to eat a half-dozen rolls without paying for a single one of them ! I'm going to try his game.

I find Husson there, who gets out the *Montparnasse*. That evening, I go out on the café-terraces and sell his paper. I get five sous for each paper sold, and that puts a little butter on your bread ! Then, too, they often ask me to show my bosom for ten sous.

They don't have to beg me to do it !

The Rotonde has just opened up an annex ; so I

KIKI PAINTING

don't go to the Parnasse Bar so much as I used to ; I like bright lights and pictures on the wall.   And besides at the Rotonde, there's always a nutty crowd.

I have a stand-in with the washroom woman, who lets me eat with her.   She's well taken care of, for Brosset sees to it that she does a good business !   The cooks heat water for me, and I take my bath in the washrooms. What's the difference, anyway ; it's just like home there !

XVIII

KISLING

There's a new customer who looks very sunburned. He has a bang on his forehead, and he's sort of hard-boiled, and I don't dare look at him very much, for I've just heard him say to the manager : "Who's the new whore ?"

I don't like that.

I don't say anything, because I'm a little bit afraid of him, but I don't lose any time in telling my friend about it. "That's Kisling", he says, admiringly.

And then, they introduce me to Kisling !

When he sees me close up, on the terrace, he begins asking me all sorts of questions, calling me a tart and a syphilitic old bitch, all in the friendliest way you could imagine.

I'm insulted, and make up my mind not to talk to him.

Too bad ! Because I like him !

Photo Thérèse Treize

ON A PICNIC NEAR CHATILLON

XIX

POSING

Kisling's promised not to bawl me out any more. He's given me a contract for three months. But most of the time, I'm a mess as a model. He yells out at the top of his voice to make me laugh, or else—makes all sorts of funny noises, and we try to see who can outdo the other. That's the only thing that can hand me a laugh any more ! And after all, he's so nice : I swipe his soap and his tooth-paste, and he never says a word : he's the swellest guy in the world !

A great little playmate !

Zborowski climbs the stairs several times in the course of the morning, just to get an eyeful and see how things are coming along.

Fels also comes in. I'm not afraid of him. He looks me over as if I were a hunk of beef in front of a butcher-shop. He's got a smile that says a lot and a pair of wicked eyes. He sees what he's looking at !

XX

1922

FOUJITA

I also posed for Foujita.

The thing that astonished him about me was the lack of hair on my sexual parts.   He often used to come over and put his nose above the spot to see—if the hair hadn't started to sprout while I'd been posing.   Then, he'd pipe up with that thin little voice of his : "That's ve' funny—no hairs !   Why your feet so dirty ?"

I had a mania for going around in my bare feet, and he'd forgotten to lay down any rugs !

When he'd sold a picture for which I'd posed, he would give me two or three hundred francs.   Other

I POSE . . .

times, he liked to roll a forty-sou piece as far as he could, and you should have seen me fly after it ! But I was simply crazy about him ! He was charming. I often used to drop in and watch him work.

He'd ask me to sing *Louise*, and then, I'd give an imitation of an orchestra ; there was one little air on the flute that went over big. He would burst out laughing, and say again : "That's ve' funny !"

Another good kid, simple and nice.

XXI

MAN RAY

I've become acquainted with an American who makes the nicest photographs. I'm going to pose for him. He has an accent that I like and a kind of mysterious way with him.

He says to me : "Kiki, don't look at me like that ! You upset me . . . !"

I've been to the movies to see *"La Dame aux Camélias."* There we were, hand in hand, and Wassilieff (I don't know her very well) was along. She looked at us as if she understood.

Now, he's my lover. The other one's going away, and I can't make up my mind to go with him.

He goes.

I stay !

I go on living the same old life.

My new friend is not rich, but we have something to eat whenever mealtime comes around, at Delmas', at Bretelle's, or at Rosalie's.

He speaks just enough French to make himself understood ; he photographs folks in the hotel room where we live, and at night, I lie stretched out on the bed while he works in the dark. I can see his face over the little red light, and he looks like the devil himself ; I am so on pins and needles that I can't wait for him to get through. We hang out with a crowd called Dadaists and some called Surréalistes—for my part, I don't see much difference between them ! There is Tristan Tzara, Breton, Philippe Soupault, Aragon, Max Ernst, Paul Eluard, etc. . .

Our nights are spent in talking, which doesn't bore me very much, even if I don't know what it's all about.

I have a great admiration for his art ; he makes pretty photos. The one that strikes me most is the

ON A WICKER CHAISE LOUNGE IN AN EARLY MAN RAY PHOTO OF KIKI, 1921

photo of the Marquise Cassati, taken through a glass bowl filled with water and leaves. The Marquise had moved a little, and this produced an extraordinary effect.

He received, I want to tell you, in this simple little hotel room, all the aristocracy and the most famous people of the day.

Man Ray has never stopped being a painter as well as a photographer. His paintings, too, are quite extraordinary. Just as in his photos, there are only three colors in his painting : black, white, grey. What drives May Ray to despair is that I have a nigger's tastes : I'm too fond of flashy colors !

And yet, he loves the black race . . .

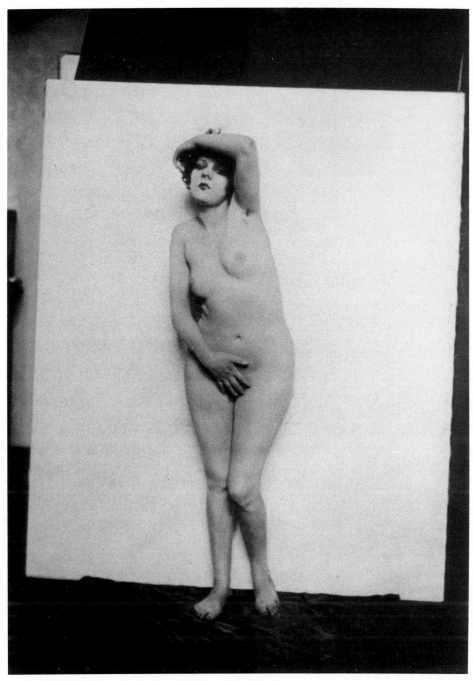

STANDING BEFORE A MAKESHIFT WHITE BACKDROP IN A *1921* PHOTO

XXII

THE JOCKEY

We've started off a new little night-club that looks like it's going to be a bright-light spot. It's called the "Jockey", because Miller, who's interested in it, is a jockey. Hiler, the painter, is at the piano ; and he's some player. Hiler is a guy who doesn't show his hand. He puts on a far-away look to help him get by, and hides behind his big ears. It is to him that we owe the pretty decorations. The walls are covered with the weirdest sort of posters you could imagine ; and every night, we're just like one big family there. Everybody drinks a lot, and everybody's happy. Scads of Americans, and what kids they are !

Every customer has a right to do his stuff. There's one big Russian there, very fat and stocky, who absolutely insists upon putting on national dances. All he can do is squat, and somebody has to take him under the arms to help him get on his feet again. There's also the pretty Floriane, who does the naughty-naughty dances that go over so big . . . and others besides. Months and years pass, and the Jockey's still the rage, the one big-time attraction of the Quarter. There are new bosses, Daddy Londish, who is very nice, and Henri, the new manager. He has as good a time as the customers do. If there's a free-for-all, everybody's in the right ! He never likes to contradict any one, but he's a swell boxer just the same. If you ask me, I think he's a knockout !

They allow the performers to pass the hat. There's one singer called "Chiffon". She's full of life, but is always a little behind the piano, which drives the orchestra crazy. She also has a cute little lisp ! Oh, yes . . . she has something else that makes a hit ! She has . . . well, she's a little under four feet eleven, and I don't mean in her stocking feet ! But Chiffon is some girl, and everybody's crazy about her.

Now, there are some café-singers, the kind that think they're just too Spanish for words, don't you know ? with heavy legs and light hips—as Chiffon says, they're the—the sh—. We show them where to head in, Chiffon and me. We see that everybody makes as much noise as possible while their number's on. The new ones don't go over very big, because everybody feels that they're cutting in. For my part, I can't sing unless I'm ginny, and I can't see how women like that can go ahead and do their stuff just as if they were sitting down to take a p—. So far as I'm concerned, I've got a good ear but a bum memory ; and it's a good thing for me my girl-friend "Treize" is with me to give me the proper hunch and act as prompter. She's the one who tomorrow will be telling me that, in my half-cocked condition the night before, I made at least twenty dates. Treize and me, we are just like that ! If either one of us gets or gives anything, whether it's a punch in the nose or something else, we always go

KIKI, 1924

fifty-fifty !   Everybody in Paris comes to the Jockey to have a good time.   All the theatre and motion-picture stars, writers, painters. . .   Van Dongen often came, and Kisling, Per Krogh, Foujita, Derain . . .

And nearly every night, Ivan Mosjoukine with the handsome eyes that made such a hit with all the ladies ! They called him "Kean", after a picture that was showing then . . .   Jacques Catelain also came, dropping his nice, bashful eyes, and what pretty women, what gowns !

XXIII

NEW YORK

I'm going to America.

I'm all upset.   I'm afraid New York won't be the way it looks in the movies.

I'm traveling on an English boat, and there's nothing exciting about that !   There are three of us women in the same cabin.   When I went in to go to bed the first night, one of them was sleeping on her back with her mouth open.   She was as yellow as a lemon, with white hair and teeth that stuck out into the middle of the stateroom.   The other one was sleeping and snoring away.   She had drawn her curtains.   My own bunk was so high up that I couldn't hoist myself into it, and so, I went out to sleep in the passageway.   When I came in the next morning at seven o'clock, they gave me a couple of dirty looks, but I explained to them that there wasn't any ladder.   It's a terrible bore in the mornings.   The one with the long teeth spends an hour in brushing them, and then, it's the other one's turn. They get real friendly with me, and I show them my own teeth, just to prove that I'm a good sport.

I drink a lot of champagne.   My legs feel heavy, but I'm not seasick.   But I don't feel like having anything in the morning except a cup of coffee.   I think of Montparnasse, and it makes me blue.   All that stretch of water out there, it gives me the creeps, especially when the sea is angry.

The boat creaks and groans, and we come to a stop every so often on account of the fog.

We get in at night.

I can't wait for day to come so that I can go out for a walk.   I put up at the Hotel Lafayette, a French hotel, where I had some good wine to drink.   It made me think of my own Paris ; the only thing was, it lost

KIKI'S DRAWING OF A NEW YORK STREET SCENE, 1923

its taste on account of the cups they served it in.

I went to the movies almost every afternoon. The mornings I spent on the bus, for I could see all New York that way. Folks there don't bother much about you ; you can walk along the street without having to worry about being picked up by the law.

I didn't make any pictures for Paramount. I went down there for a try-out, but before going on inside the studio, I wanted to touch up my hair. When I found I'd forgotten my comb, I was fighting mad, and so, what did I do but traipse all the way back home again. Oh, well, maybe I'm better off the way it was ! It's much nicer to go to movies than to make them. I remember, the first time I tried acting for the movies in France, I came near being torn to pieces by the monkeys, for I didn't care much about them. That was in a picture called "*Galerie des monstres*". The bear wanted to lay a leg with me, and the lights blinded me.

But that, as they say, is another story !

I stayed in New York only three months.

XXIV

VILLEFRANCHE 1925

Here I am at Villefranche.

It's February, and it's raining, and I'm a little under the weather.

I miss my Jockey Club.

They've given me a nice room on the fourth floor. I'm staying with a girl-friend.   We go down to the hotel bar, and there, we find some American sailors.   I get upstage, and remark : "I'm a little bit afraid of those big bruisers !"   Then, I begin to feel at home in this hotel.   I meet a lot of old friends : an American girl and her brother, Jean Cocteau and some friends of his, etc. . . It begins to seem like a family party ; and by this time, all the sailors are friends of mine, too.

We begin dancing about five o'clock at night, and we end up at three in the morning. There are a number of women from Marseilles and Nice, trailing the boat to pick up their sweethearts. There are some nice whores among them, with good manners—even elegant, you might say—but a bit sloppy. When the boat leaves port, there they are, all lined up with their handkerchiefs, and how they weep ! They get up just as close as they can to the edge of the wharf, so that it will feel like they're going away with their boy-friends.

And for eight whole days, they keep it up !

They spend their days in writing letters, and in the evening, try to forget their troubles with other sailors.

Treize and Per Krohg have just arrived. They are crazy about the good-looking sailors. We've adopted five or six of 'em, and we're together all the time.

Per Krogh never gets tired of sketching sailors. For recreation, he gives me a few pinches in the rump. That tickles Treize, but it leaves me cold. I've got a behind that's proof against anything.

ON THE BALCONY OF THE WELCOME HOTEL IN VILLEFRANCHE

XXV

IN BAD WITH THE LAW

Per Krohg, Treize and a number of other friends have left for Paris. I stay behind with my girl-friend, who is eighteen.

One evening, I go to look up some sailor friends in an English bar where we never hang out. I had barely opened the door, when the boss yells at me from behind the counter : "No whores allowed here !"

I make one leap for him and shove a pile of saucers in his face. My pals butt into the scuffle, but the navy police are on the job ! We have time to beat it into another bar, but I was shadowed ; and besides, I lived in a hotel that the whole town of Villefranche was down on because it did too good a business.

The next morning, about eight, they send for me to come down. I go down to the lobby, and through the door which is half-way open, I catch sight of a red face and a policeman's uniform. The cop makes a sign for me to come along.

That's nothing in my young life.

He goes away and comes back with some guy in civvies who looks as if he's just too tired to move. This guy tells me that I'm under arrest, that he's the constable of Villefranche, and he shows me his papers.

He acted as if he was half crazy, and was so mad that he shook all over. When I didn't step quite lively enough to suit him, he said to the fellows that were with him : "Grab her, boys !" They jumped all over me, and the constable himself gave me a punch in the side of the head. I wasn't just exactly expecting that wallop, and fell over, arms first, against the constable. "A fine case we got against *you*," he says to me then, "attacking an officer !" And he kept on insulting me all the way to his office.

They turned me over to a big cop,—and a regular

cop is what I mean, with a face like a bulldog,—and he showed me the goldfish for fair. There was a big revolver on the desk, but I didn't know how to handle it.

THE BAR IN VILLEFRANCHE

XXVI

IN JAIL

They take me down into a dark cellar, where there is nothing but a board, what's left of a bicycle, and a lot of other old junk . . .

I've been there long enough to think things over plenty, when the door opens and one of my girl-friends comes in sobbing, with a basket on her arm, followed by a big copper.

When I looked at that copper's neck, my fingers twitched, I can tell you !   After that, they take me out of the cellar and take me to Nice.   I have to climb up in the black Maria, and when we get there, all I can see is big gloomy walls in front of me.

They hand me the once-over.

How many corridors ! How many doors ! They take me to my cell. A matron shows me my cot and a toilet-stool with a chain attached, and then goes away...

I'm scared stiff. It's dark ! I ask for a light and they laugh at me. I fall on my cot and cry. I haven't slept in the dark since I was four years old ! I start howling, the way a dog does at night, until the woman up above me yells down : "Cut the comedy !"

The walls are thick, but through them I can hear other women sobbing . There's one right next to me who's not as young as I am, and so, she must be more miserable.

At five in the morning, they come around and ask me what I want to eat, for they're only holding me on suspicion.

The days are long. The Easter holidays set everything back, and although they've given me another cell, I've just about come to think that I'm never going to get out of here !

I have visitors. There's one fat motherly old dame

with red cheeks who is very familiar with me and who looks after my tobacco and wine ; and at night, she slips into my cell to give me some hot chocolate.

In order to wash myself, I have to leave my basin under the faucet all night long. And my thunder-mug, which is never cleaned, stinks up the whole cell.

They take my finger-prints and look me over from head to foot for any scars that I may have.

A gentleman friend of mine has sent me a lawyer, but he acts as if he didn't believe a word I told him !

They give us an hour's recreation. Each prisoner has a little three-cornered court.

They've lent me the *Three Musketeers* to amuse myself, but I know it by now from one end to the other !

I'm going to have to tell it to the judge. The prison black Maria comes to pick us up : four women and nine men, and a couple of cops that smell like garlic. But it's not my turn yet, and back I go to jail. That's hard luck ! The hardest part of the day for me is when night comes, and my cell gets dark, and I can see just

KIKI'S PAINTING OF SAILORS AND A PROSTITUTE, 1929

a tiny speck of colored light on the ceiling. There's a railway station nearby, and I can hear the trains whistling . . . and all this time, the prison seems to be asleep... a sleeping dungeon !

I've been here for twelve days, and tomorrow, I go to court. My lawyer has promised to get me out, but he tells me they've got some case against me—resisting an officer, sloughing a cop : that generally means six months in prison at the very least. If I'm sent over, I'm going to kill myself. I don't think I'll ever be able to forget, not for years, the hate I feel inside myself at this minute !

XXVII

TELLING IT TO THE JUDGE

I've got to tell it to the judge today.

"Judge!" Who has the right to judge ?

I've got my smelling-salts in my hand. I'm very weak ; I've lost ten pounds in thirteen days. I climb back up into the same old black Maria. I never like the smell of it ! I meet some fellows who were with me the other day. You wouldn't recognize them. I wonder if they feel the same way about me ?

The cop wants me to sit on his lap. He must think he's doing me a favor. I'd prefer the lap of any gazebo there !

Here we are.

A full house.   I'll come up about noon.

On the floor is some fellow groaning, while others are standing around holding him.   He's having an epileptic fit.   That makes a hit with the judges.   The poor guy had tampered a little with his chauffeur's license !   The aisle is so narrow that, when they call me, I'm going to have to straddle over that fellow's body.

It's my turn.   I'm so ashamed, I blush all over and can't see what I'm doing !   My lawyer whispers to me to keep still and look innocent !   I don't answer ; I can't say anything.

My gentleman friend is here, as a character witness, and he's got some of his buddies with him.   It makes me sad to see him under such circumstances, and I start to cry.   Just before me is an old woman who has stolen a little gold basket-work cross.   She cries, and they let her off.   Then, it's a big girl's turn, with a clipped head ; she's from the Public Aid, and she has no lawyer.   A gentleman with whom she was sleeping has lost his pocket-book and is accusing her.

IN COURT

Three months ! Her poor sad little face is a sight to see.

Here's a skinny little brunette, a fifteen-year-old flapper with a Marseilles accent. She's been in a battle with a dick from the morals squad. She threatens to get him ! and tells the judge that they pinched her because she wouldn't play along with the "higher-ups". Two months in prison ! She whispers to me, with that accent of hers : "Sh— ! Two months more for crab-hunting !" . . . It's my turn !

I don't care much about them, nor they about me.

A judge with a white beard, the one in the middle, asks me if I'd been drinking. I tell him certainly not ! He tells me that what I did was all the more inexcusable. Pulling at his beard, he adds that my gentleman friend is in the room ! I looked at my friend, and I saw that if he had had a revolver, the judge would have stopped pulling at his beard pretty quick.

The constable is here to swear that I struck and insulted him. One of the witnesses he had brought in says, with a cute little accent : "Oh, yes, she handed him a nice one" ; but the guy from the bar, who had not showed up, had made a statement to the effect that it was he who had insulted me first, that he had been in the wrong, and that if the expenses of the case were paid, he was willing to withdraw his complaint ! That grand sailor boy who was with me at the time had gone around taking up a collection on all the boats, and all his friends had got so worked up about it that they had chipped in twenty-five thousand francs to buy my freedom for me ! But that s— of a b— of a constable was bound I wasn't going to be let off ; he was going to make me eat beans for at least six months.

Then my lawyer spoke up. He told the judge that I was a little bit cracked, and showed certificates to prove that I had nervous trouble.

The hardest part was when my lawyer turned to me and said : "Thank these gentlemen here !"

That was a hard one for me !

And here I am, free again !

I went to Paris, and a few evenings later, I was singing a song at the Jockey Club, a song that became rather popular on account of me, "*les Filles de Cama-ret*". And of course, I had to run around to see my dear old Dôme, and Daddy Chambon, who said to me : "Ah ! there you are, you big girl, you !" And he didn't forget to give me a good slap on the rump ! And I saw Ernest again, looking more like a first-communion lad and friendlier than ever ; and I wondered if he was still a virgin. Ah ! Montparnasse ! how I needed you to forget !

Pierre Prévert, 1928

KIKI AND TREIZE, SHOWING HER PET MOUSE, IN PIERRE PRÉVERT'S *PARIS LA BELLE*, 1928

XXVIII

JEAN COCTEAU

The first time that I saw Cocteau was at Man Ray's, where he had come to have his photograph made. He had put on a pair of woolen gloves colored red, white and black. I thought at first that he must have come to have his gloves photographed !

He took advantage of the occasion to have his hair photographed and his eyes too, which are restless but pleasant. He has eyes like a pair of diamonds . . .

I have met Cocteau many times, and each time I like him better. He is so charming, and so simple that when I'm with him I feel as though I've known him all my life. I made a portrait of him from memory, which

KIKI PAINTED AN ELEGANT JEAN COCTEAU

wasn't so bad some folks thought, and which was sold in London.

I saw him again at exhibits, at the Bœuf sur le Toit, rue Boissy d'Anglas, where Doucet used to read love stories, acting them out so divinely.

In 1925, we found ourselves in the same hotel in Villefranche. He has, like me, a great passion for anything that comes from the sea. We used to meet every evening in the little hotel bar, where we enjoyed watching the sailors and the whores. Jean has made some pretty drawings from this period. He sent me a most amusing letter once from Villefranche, but unfortunately, it is a little bit too daring to be reproduced here ! Are there any daring things ?

In this letter, he wrote to me like the proprietor of a house to a lady boarder . . . It is a letter filled with remonstrances and good advice.

This brings us down to 1929. I saw my good friend Jean Cocteau on other occasions. He often used to come of an evening to listen to me sing at the Bœuf, rue de Penthièvre. His presence gave me more self-confidence. What's more, I can see that all his friends around him are charmed by his manners and his wit ; they are in love with him. He gave me a necklace fit for a queen.

XXIX

MONTPARNASSE TODAY

Here I am, back in Montparnasse, which to me is the land of liberty. As I see it, I can cut up all I want to here, without being afraid of having to go eat beans again.

Folks here are broad-minded, and what would be a crime anywhere else is simply a little false pass.

Montparnasse, so picturesque, so colorful ! All the peoples of the earth have come here to pitch their tents; and yet, it's all just like one big family.

In the morning, you can see young fellows in wide trousers and fresh-cheeked young girls on their way to the art-schools, to Watteau's, to Colarossi's, to the Grande

Photo Man Ray

Chaumière, etc . . . Later, the café-terraces begin to fill up, and pretty Americans eating oatmeal can be seen sitting side by side the French *picons-citron*. The crowd goes to look for a ray of sunlight at the cafés. The models meet one another there. They're true to their trade : Aïcha ; Bouboule ; Clara . . . There are few as nice as they left any more ! In the evening, I meet my little playmates once more : Foujita and the pretty Youki ; Derain, who laughs at his own stories ; Kisling with his Tom Mix shirts and his wife who has the gayest laugh in Paris. There is Desnos, who is all fussed up because a number of persons have asked him to do something for them ; that gives the impression that he's a fast-liver. And Sessue-Hayakawa, drawing away on his little old pipe without batting an eye, and Fernande, who smiles and bustles around and makes more noise and commotion by herself alone than a banquet with a hundred and ten plates. She has stunning eyes, eyes that see darned far. She makes up, with Marga, "13", Edouard, Ramond, Arbens and a lot of other pals that I'll never forget but can't mention here because there are too many of'em, a swell little crowd and one that you see a good deal of around Montparnasse.

There is Man Ray, who always seems to be looking into little pieces of glass, or else, dreaming about some new-fangled sort of photographic apparatus.

There's Lucy, and there's Pascin, with his derby sinking further and further down over his ear. He talks very low and gives his little gang the once-over. He's an awful kidder, but he's got a big heart in spite of his jokes ; you can tell that from his eye. He's as good as gold.

To make a long story short, Montparnasse is a village that is as round as a circus. You get into it you don't know just how, but getting out again is not so easy !

There are people who have got off by accident at the Vavin subway station, and who have never left the district again, have stayed there all their lives. As for middle class citizens who happen to pass through, they don't know what it is all about, and they are so frightened out of their wits that they don't stay there any longer than they have to ! Montparnasse runs the Berlitz School a close second in languages. Since I have come to Montparnasse, I'm going to have to talk even Chinese—but I'm not giving up.

In the evening, at aperitive-time, you meet a gang of good fellows. The big problem is where to go for dinner. Sometimes you go to the Djiguites, where you are waited on by what are supposed to be Russian Princesses ; or else, you go to a Scandinavian restaurant but that's not so hot if you ask me. Sometimes, you meet the gang at ten or twelve at the Coupole bar. That's where the wisecracks begin to fly and Derain gets off his jokes. One time, when he must have had a good dinner, he took it into his head to stick his foot into the rounds of the bar-stools, and proceeded to give the poor chaps who clung to them a ride, jolting them along over the floor.

It is too bad the little wine-shops where one used to be able to get so nice a meal have all disappeared.

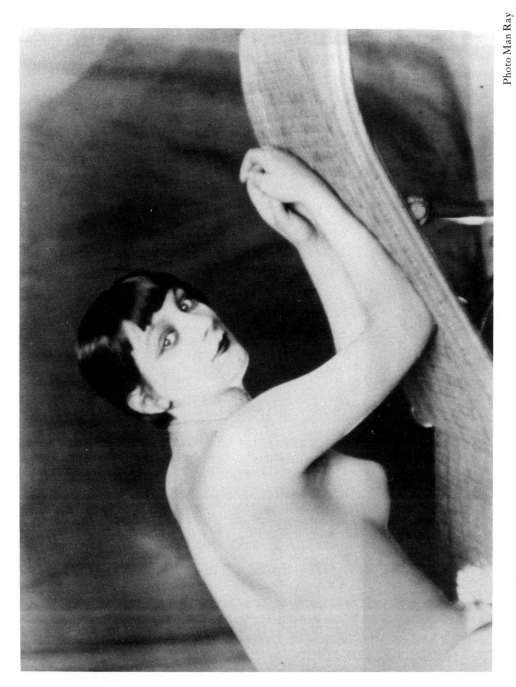

ON A WICKER CHAISE LOUNGE SEEN OFTEN IN MAN RAY'S PHOTOGRAPHS

Photo Man Ray

To find something to do after dinner is not so hard ; all you have to do is choose !

There are plenty of dancing places, and very often, I made the rounds of them all a number of times in one night. Sometimes, there are parties, like the ones at Foujita's, where Robert Desnos played old records for us which he had bought with Youki at the Flea Market, back in the days when Mercadier and Paulus were singing.

Sometimes, the crowd bumps into Pascin, who takes everybody home with him. He wrestles with bottles and corkscrews. Often, his models are there, models of all shades ! He is so glad to see a lot of folks around him.

He sometimes gives parties in the country, takes whole caravans out with him ! There often used to be as many as forty and fifty around to listen to his stories : André Salmon ; Nils Dardels and his story about the little rabbit ; Aïcha ; Gallibert ; Lucy ; Simone ; Zborowski ; Soutine ; and a lot of other good fellows.

And then, there are the dance halls !

The Bal de la Horde, the Bal Russe, and especially the Bal Suedois at the Académie Watteau. I never miss out on them ; you can have a better time there than any place else, and I have seen some Scandinavians that were as jolly as anybody.

There are the movie evenings, when you go to the 4 Colonnes, rue de la Gaité, or to Bobino's.

Some evenings, I must say, they tried to turn me aside from the path of duty and take me to Montmartre.

But I refused to be a deserter.

KIKI,
Montparnasse, 1929.

KIKI TALKS OPENLY TO YOU

Ici Paris Hebdo *July—August 1950*

"Kiki vous parle sans pose" appeared in three install-
ments in the Paris newspaper Ici Paris *on July 31, August*
7, and in the weekend edition entitled Ici Paris Hebdo, *Au-*
gust 14, 1950. They cover the years before Alice became
Kiki: her childhood, her early days in Paris, and the first
years at the Café de La Rotonde. They add new details to
some incidents touched on only briefly in the earlier mem-
oirs and also add new stories and comments. The picture
they paint is much harsher as she comments emotionally on
the misery in her childhood and reflects on the difference not
only between the Paris of pre-Depression 1929 and the
Paris of postwar 1950, but also between a twenty-eight-year-
old Kiki at the height of her creativity, sensuality, and fame,
and a fifty-year-old Kiki, who was battling illness, drink,
and drugs and would die just three years later. But as al-
ways, she can make us cry and laugh at an appalling child-
hood and make us admire even more the woman who
survived it to become Kiki.

Photo Man Ray

MY CHILDHOOD

I was born the 2nd of October 1901 in a pretty little corner of Burgundy.

My mother was 18 years old and her lover, my father, 19. She was poor, he was rich; both were handsome.

Sometime later, my father was forced by his father and mother to make an advantageous marriage with a rich farmer's daughter.

As for my mother, she hid her delicate condition from her father until the last moment. I was not a welcome arrival!

When I announced I was coming, my mother was a few meters from our house. The pains forced her to sit down on the edge of the sidewalk.

My godfather, who was coming to get the latest

news, got the picture; he picked my mother up in his arms and carried her to her bed.

Since he was a bootlegger, he got her really plastered! As for me, I profited from it; I arrived tipsy.

As soon as I could walk and talk, I never left my god-father's side.

In addition to his bootleg alcohol, he drove a cart pulled by an old horse. He was in charge of collecting the garbage, which we dumped in a field out in the country-side.

Me, I completed the picture. My bottom spread out on the rags and scrap iron. I was happy and rummaged around with delight. Everything is relative. I played Alice in Wonderland! And I found such wonderful things there!

And afterwards, I didn't let myself be beaten down for it.

My godfather loved to have a glass or two, and since I was already advanced for my age, he dragged me to all the bistros. I was allowed to have my glass of fruit syrup, and I drank what was left at the bottom of their glasses!

At this time they were drinking the real Pernod. Then I climbed up on the marble tabletop and began my song.

Afterward, I didn't forget to pass the hat.

I already cared about how I looked! It seemed—and I remember it—that I couldn't sing my ballads without paying attention to my knees. If they were too dirty, I spit on them and tried to clean them with the bottom of my apron, which made two white circles on a gray background; and I pulled down my knickers down so the lace trim stuck out and covered them.

MY GOOD GRANDMOTHER

I was brought up by my grandmother, who in addition to me had collected Marcel, Pierre, and Jean, the three children of an aunt who had died, and Madeleine, one of the two daughters of another aunt, my aunt Laure.

Madeleine was redheaded. Her mother didn't like her very much because of the color of her hair and her resemblance to her father who was long gone and unlamented. So she had simply shipped this poor Madeleine to grandmother along with five francs per month, which anyway she often forgot to send. You could have put a sign on the door: "The House of the Six Reunited Bastards."

My mother was in Paris. Grandmother wore herself out feeding all these young starving mouths. She must

KIKI, *THE CHURCH TOWER* (*SAINT-NICOLAS IN CHATILLON*), 1926

have suffered a lot of hardships! Often she screamed at us, but we screamed back even louder.

The neighbors criticized her for her weakness; and in order to make them think that she beat us sometimes, she would very conspicuously take the handle of the broom . . . and bang it on the table. The six kids tried to bawl as if they were being skinned alive. Then the neighbors would say to my grandmother, "My poor Marie! You must have courage! You should turn them all over to Public Assistance." Then grandmother would get red with anger, "I will raise my bastards, it's nobody else's business. It's the jerks their fathers who should be blamed."

The only father still living was mine and he could not disavow me. We resembled each other that much.

As chance would have it, he lived in a pretty, rich-looking house not far from our miserable one.

The only justice that the Good Lord provided, and which soothed the pride of a poor little girl, was what I heard people say about the daughter that my father had with his wife: "There is no other way to put it, they are really two sisters. One is just as ugly as the other." In the Burgundian dialect *"peute"* means *"ugly."*

Obviously we couldn't meet without wanting to kill each other, and when we fought, she said, "I am going to tell my father."

"I don't give a damn," I would say, "he's my father too." Since I was older than she, it seemed to me I should have more rights to say whose father he should be.

She had her revenge on holidays. My cousins and I always had our hair cut very short, which didn't keep the "cooties" from camping out there. There were one or two holidays in the year, and my grandmother let us grow our hair out for several weeks to prepare for them.

Poor dear grandmother! She understood our humiliation very well, and she knew that we looked with heavy hearts at the other little girls with their long hair held back with ribbons and large bows.

For me, by pulling and Vaselining my hair, I succeeded in having it hold a little ribbon that cost one *sous* per meter. It was an attempt to be a little darling, but I ended up looking like a bunch of salad greens.

But my sorrow was lessened because for those days my grandmother, instead of washing our hair with gasoline, gave us a rubdown with rum or marc. This didn't smell as bad, but our little animals liked it as much as we did. They got happily drunk, and we felt as if there were twice as many of them.

What counts when you are a kid is to have curly hair and a beautiful braid! With my thin and short hair, I felt I was poor, despised, and belittled! Maybe I put my pride in the wrong place, but I didn't have many things in my physique to raise my spirits or make me forget that I was not a shining star.

When you meet an ugly and neglected little girl with her head shaved like an egg, don't laugh: pitiful hair makes grown-ups laugh but little ones cry.

A DISTURBING FATHER

My father was a big dealer in wood and charcoal; he had a farm. He was a bigwig in town.

I would sometimes run into him on the road. Then my heart would begin to pound. He always wanted to take me into the woods with him. But my grandmother had terrorized me! She told me, "If you go with him, he will kill you like the others." And it is true that I had two sisters who had died in suspicious circumstances.

When I was very young, something like that very nearly happened to me. He was at our house, and he sent my mother to buy some wine. When she came back, I had swallowed a glass of milk and was very sick. Fortunately, my grandmother arrived, just as I started to turn completely black! She made me throw up immediately and I hung onto life.

Yet I had a great desire to follow him into the woods. Maybe, instead of doing harm to me, he would simply embrace me like a father embraces his little daughter. No one knows what sorrow fills the heart of a child who doesn't have a father, whose mother is far away, and whose only tenderness in life comes from a grandmother.

Dear old grandmother! Yours is the only memory that I evoke with emotion. The kisses from your wrinkled face and the caresses from your reddened hands are the only sweet things from my childhood.

KIKI'S PAINTING *WASHERWOMAN* EVOKES HER CHILDHOOD

THE DEATH OF GRANDFATHER

My grandfather worked on the roads. He broke up stones for the roads! Poor grandfather! I do not have very good memories of you.

He was it seems a very honest man, but he was very strict. I was scared of him, and I remember very little about him except for his death throes, because it was I who helped him as he was dying. When I think of it, I begin to tremble all over. How could they have had the idea to leave a little girl of nine, impressionable and sensitive as I was, face to face with a dying person.

Grandmother, who had to go to work, put a napkin in my hands with the instructions to wipe off the slobber that ran down his beard, and the poor old man begged me to bring him his boots so he could polish them. Then I understood that he wanted to say, "I am preparing myself for the big journey."

My grandfather's sister lived about two hours from us. When he was about to draw his last breath, a neighbor lady went to get her. It was the middle of the night but she came immediately, and I remember her arrival, her snuffbox in her hand. "Sometimes," she said, "they attack me along the road." Yet she wasn't very scared, she was as big as a *gendarme* and ate and drank copiously.

Since we were very poor, we lived in one big room with an alcove.

After shedding some tears, my aunt Laure decided nonetheless that we should go to bed. The gang of kids and my grandmother stretched out in the bed in the alcove, and my Aunt Laure, very naturally, took a chair, put it against the bed and jamming poor grandfather in, lay down fully dressed next to the dead body.

Death among poor people is not a catastrophe as it is among the rich, and when you have slaved all your life and barely succeeded in feeding yourself, the final departure is considered a deliverance.

MY ARRIVAL IN PARIS

When I was twelve, my mother had me come to
Paris. It was not with the idea of giving me a lot of educa-
tion, but since I was going to learn the trade of linotypist,
I had at least to know vaguely how to spell. This was the
trade that my mother had practiced since she was young,
and she was in Paris with a M. Gaston, who was her boss.

For one year they stuck me in the public school on
rue Vaugirard. I must not have seemed very intelligent,
and the school mistress sat me with the kids who were
seven and eight years old. At the end of the year, I didn't
know much more than when I entered.

As soon as my thirteenth year and one day arrived, it
was time to earn my living! They put me in a bookbind-
ing shop. I began to make deliveries. If it was for this, it

ON VACATION IN THE SOUTH, KIKI GREETS THE SUN

was not worth the trouble to have me learn how to spell!

I was loaded down like a donkey, wearing a jacket of pleated sateen tied up at the waist; and to finish off the costume, a splendid pair of button-up boots in a beautiful yellow with the ankle part of gray cloth. Since I was always very thin, both of my calves could have fitted easily into the same upper part of one boot. Then *La Presse* and *Le Bonnet Rouge*, both newspapers of that time, shared the job. One wedged my calf and the other did what it could to keep the end of the shoe from bending too much. Because I forgot to tell you that the boots were size 39 or 40 and at that time I took a size 34. Obviously I had a very funny awkward walk but to tell the truth, I was proud of myself anyway. At this time boots like these were worn by kept women. The one who had thrown this pair in the trash, where my mother found them, must have been a real *gendarme*, around forty years old, with big tits and a real rear end! I think that if she returned to earth, such a one from the Belle Epoque, it is hard to believe that a man would buy such extravagant things for her.

It is true that at this time a handsome male had a beautiful pair of mustaches and hair down to his belly. In any case, at thirteen, when I saw a man with a beautiful flowing beard spreading out over a lavalliere tie, my heart started to beat quickly. And if he had a belly, I admired him unreservedly. He could only have been a poet, painter, or actor. Beyond these three professions, I was not interested in any other mortal being.

MISERABLE FLOWERS

Every Saturday, I went to friends who lived on rue Mouffetard and were flower sellers.

Sunday, we were up at 5 A.M. to go to Les Halles to buy flowers cheaply. The flowers that were more or less dead ended up in our hands and it was a big job. They were broken, withered and the bottom of the barrel! We were a real bunch of crooks!

Let's go! A pink bath for this one and a matchstick to replace the missing stem and everything held together with wire and a little bit of greenery. And when the clock struck ten the whole troupe was in front of Eglise St. Medard [on rue Mouffetard] and were among the ones who yell the loudest. We would roll our eyes to try to attract customers away from the competition.

KIKI PLAYS PROSTITUTE TO MAN RAY'S CLIENT

Everything worked very well. The next Sunday, the client who noticed that in all the bouquets there were stems of all kinds simply went to another seller. Since the family of our friends was blessed with three girls and two guys, a grandmother and me, you understand that we had a lot of sales before finally losing a client. But even so I was not completely at ease about this and was very conscious of the faults of each bouquet. I preferred to palm them off on women clients! It was less dangerous.

Even so, I was already flirting with the men! It was truly pretentious of me to think that my face attracted them. From time to time they relieved me of my illusions. What made me mad was when they looked at my profile and shouted, "Hey sister, spear me that wedge of brie!" It's true that I had one of those large noses that my thinness made seem even more pointed.

To top off my misfortune, they dressed me from the flea market. But I avenged myself with jewelry; every strand of my hair was held back with small combs with shiny multicolored stones. I was a real basket peddler, from the neigborhoods out by the old Paris walls.

IN TROUBLED WATERS

Like all good workers my mother took a bath every Sunday. When I arrived from the country, she took me with her to clean me up a bit.

To make it cheaper, we took our own towels and soap, and that was the cause of the whole uproar. If we had at least taken the soap that they sell there, this little piece of pink nougat which floats on the surface, nothing would have happened. So my mother and I entered and asked for a single bath. At the questioning glance of the cabin attendant, my mother put on an innocent look and answered, "It's for my big daughter. She has never taken a bath in Paris, and I am going with her." Once in the cabin, my mother obviously took advantage of the situation, undressed and took her bath with me. But here came the brave Marseille soap that sank to the bottom and I, who was a novice in accidents like this, put my foot on it. I slipped and just had time to hang onto a cord that I found in my hand to keep me from falling. Unfortunately, that was the bell to summon the attendant! And it was she who opened the door, came in, and asked what had happened.

My mother froze like a pillar of salt! She managed to get her mouth going to answer that there was nothing wrong. I don't have to tell you what happened next. She started to call me an incalculable number of names that made me hurt in the little part of me they call the heart, "I have dishonored her. She will never dare go out again, and she will be shamed in the neighborhood when they find out about such economizing. Imbecile, peasant, country bumpkin," . . . and I won't go on. . . .

Finally she got dressed, gave me six *sous* for the tip and left me in complete disarray, telling me, "Go on take care of yourself, idiot!"

If she could have understood the sad state of my spirit! She never was a mother to me, and yet I loved her

A PHOTO TAKEN IN THE SOUTH

with all the affection that a small being who is alone in the world can have, like a poor battered dog who comes to lick the hands of his master.

I was extremely sensitive and tense, and my mother was too young, too hard! I never dared say the word, "mama." I thought that I didn't deserve it, and when by chance we went to some friends of my mother where they had children, I saw them hugged, kissed, and coaxed by their mother. When I heard them say, "Mama dear," it seemed as if my heart would crack: I was embarrassed, blushing, and I didn't dare look at my mother.

Yet sometimes I didn't feel that she was completely indifferent. Perhaps I should have acted on my feelings and followed the desire that I had to climb on her knees, to kiss her. But I couldn't. She immediately froze me with an ironic remark, not realizing that I was so hurt and that one single human look would have made me explode.

I would have let flow all my pain and my desire to be able to say "mama," since I had never been permitted to say the word "papa" either. . . .

THE BACK ROOM AT LA ROTONDE

I often went to La Rotonde, but I wasn't allowed to walk into the large room. Père Libion, the owner, didn't accept me as a customer, basically because I didn't have a hat. But since I already had many painter friends, it bothered me to be put off.

One day Père Libion said to me: "Kiki, why don't you simply find yourself a hat? After that, you can go into the room."

I was sick not to have the right to go into the room. The first reason was that the toilets were at the back of the room, and then I wanted to mix in the first room where the painters and the artists and everyone met. There were politicians there from all over the world, and they always seemed to be plotting a revolution!

In the second room were the chess players, customers that one didn't know, and all the grand ladies of the Quarter. I wanted to see them up close, for they were all legendary. They all already had extraordinary lives. Aicha, the splendid Creole, a model much in demand; Mirielle, a very pretty dancer; Silvia, a beautiful buxom girl who one day left on vacation and never returned to Montparnasse; Germaine, a beautiful dancer with fiery eyes; Pâquerette, Mado, etc. Each one was different in personality, looks, and morality.

Photo Man Ray

MARQUIS HAT FOR
A CHRISTMAS TREE

I succeeded in finding a hat, but what a hat! in black satin, a Breton or miller type, to which, supreme elegance, and the edge was trimmed with silver chenille like you find on Christmas trees. I shaped it like a "marquis" hat and stuck it on my head. Luckily I had ears to keep it from descending too far. I must have looked like a marquis who had lost his wig!

As for my blouses, if you think I made them different on purpose, it was really that I was naive! I found an enormous catalog of lace samples in a trash can. So I pinned one or two each in the neckline of my jacket. People said, "Oh! Kiki, what pretty blouses you have!" I lowered my eyes modestly to excuse myself for having such beautiful things. But I was a little proud, and I trembled at the idea that they would want to look up close.

I now understand that no one was fooled, but in those times, everyone had an infinite amount of goodwill. Nobody ever let slip the slightest joke about my blouses, and even less about my hat.

After all, knowing that it was funny didn't bother me at all. To be able to enter the Rotonde, I was ready to march in on my head.

LA ROTONDE, MEETING PLACE

A very colorful mass of people was swarming in there; I couldn't take my eyes off of them. My eyes opened wide at this mélange of mercenary females, models, bourgeoisie full of curiosity, politicians, artists full of faith and passion, freeloading painters, etc. The whole world was there. It was colorful and musical.

Père Libion, as we called the owner, couldn't look at me without laughing. But I now had the right to enter the rooms, thanks to that memorable hat. Ah! They recognized me from far away.

And I, I had found my true milieu! The painters adopted me. End of sadnesses. I still often went hungry, but the good fun made me forget all that. I regained my healthy Burgundian cheerfulness.

KIKI, *WOMAN FIXING HER HAIR*, 1926

Nothing surprised me anymore. I remember one time Utrillo, who had managed to escape from his house, came directly to the old Rotonde. He installed himself in front of me and, still talking, began to make my portrait. Me, I was so frozen in my pose that you would think I was stuffed. After 10 minutes, he put down his pencil and paper, and I looked at it. Oh! Astonishment. I see a pretty house in the country with a little garden. When I think about it now, I believe that I understand better. I am, and I will remain, a pure-blooded country person, as my mother said with despair. I will always have dirt in my shoes. "Country bumpkin you are and country bumpkin you will remain," she told me, believing she hurt me. My land, I will never repudiate you. And I think that if one day this land disappears, my health will leave with it.

I have done really stupid things along the way, I have felt my health disappearing little by little, but always the idea of my country has saved me at the last moment; a few days in the pure air of my native countryside is sufficient for me to recover.

CLEANING OUT PÉRE LIBION

This blessed Rotonde, you went there as if you were going to your own home, you felt as if you were among family. Père Libion is the best of men, and he loves them, his ragtag bunch of artists!

Some really curious things took place there.

For example, around the time that they delivered the bread, a large family of hungry artists were all gathered there. The carrier brought in about twenty huge loaves which were put in a kind of willow basket close to the bar. But the breads were too long, and a good third jutted out above the top. Oh! Not for long. In the time it takes to turn your head, and Père Libion always left for several seconds at that moment, the tops of all the loaves were taken off in the blink of an eye; then, looking as if nothing had happened, everybody left with his piece of bread in his pocket. And it was always the same! Père Libion would begin to get angry, to talk of reprisals, of the police . . . and the next day it began again. . . .

Still that was nothing; you could go into any artist's studio at that time and you would always find a lot of souvenirs of La Rotonde: saucers, forks, knives, plates. . . . Whoever set up housekeeping, it was Père Libion who provided the *trousseau*.

One day two characters discovered that the supplies were stored next to the telephone. One of them had only to climb on the swinging door and pass the parcels to the other.

Finally one day Père Libion decided that they had gone too far. While the first had his back turned, perched on his door passing lots of goodies to his buddy, Libion came up silently, caught the second by the arms and moved him a little to the side; the first without turning his head continued to pass sugar, coffee, etc. Finally, he said , "OK old buddy, is this OK, eh? Is this enough?" And Père Libion replied, "Oh yes, you can come down."

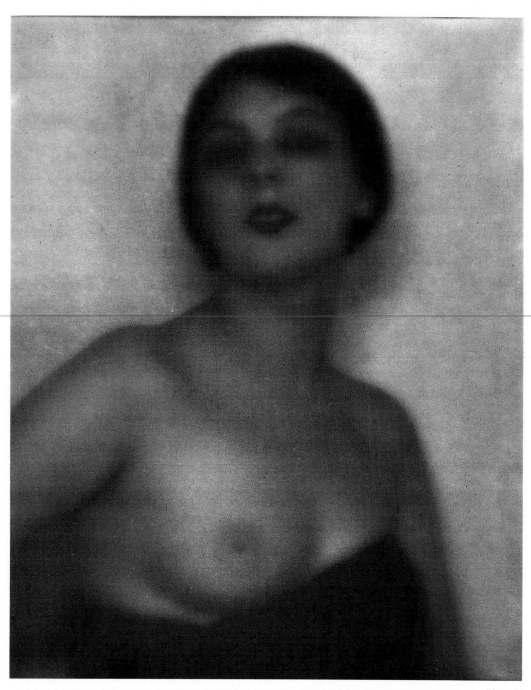

Photo Man Ray

At the sound of this voice the guy who was up top read-justed his glasses (he was myopic) and, astonished, fell down. He was green as a pear, and his buddy was also the same color.

Père Libion took each one by the ear and led them to the bar, without saying one word. Truly it was a tragic moment and everybody waited anxiously for what was coming next. Finally the owner's anger exploded.

"In the name of God, you bunch of bums! Now you will see what I am made of."

And, letting go of them, he turned his head to the barman and told him in a booming voice:

"Give them two double sandwiches and two large café-crèmes. Eat you bums."

These bums of thirty and some odd years had tears in their eyes. After all, to have done this to such a nice guy!

Ah! He knew them, "his kids" as Père Libion called them, and he really loved them! Nothing they did aston-ished him, but it was always he who had the last word.

One day a group of young painters came to invite him to celebrate the first big deal of one of their friends.

Modigliani had finally found a patron who had offered a fabulous price for one of his paintings: several hundred francs. They decided to eat it all in a tremendous meal. So Père Libion came to the dinner that evening with the whole happy group. But Modigliani was not at ease. In effect, the chairs, the knives, the glasses, the plates and even the tables, Père Libion recognized as his. He got up, didn't say anything, and left! Modigliani began to berate his buddies:

"You bunch of cretins! Why did you have to bring him here? I also love him as much as you do, but if I did not invite him, it is because of all these dishes which I have taken from him."

They looked at each other in anguish. Several minutes passed, no one wanted to eat any longer. Then the door opened. All eyes turned in that direction and what did they see: Père Libion had returned, dragging his feet, his arms full of bottles:

"Only the wine wasn't from me, so I went to get it. Let's go, to the table, I am as hungry as a wolf."

You will surely have trouble believing that these are

not made-up stories. But I assure you that I have exaggerated nothing. Moreover, if you question those who frequented La Rotonde at that time, they will tell you the same stories as I have.

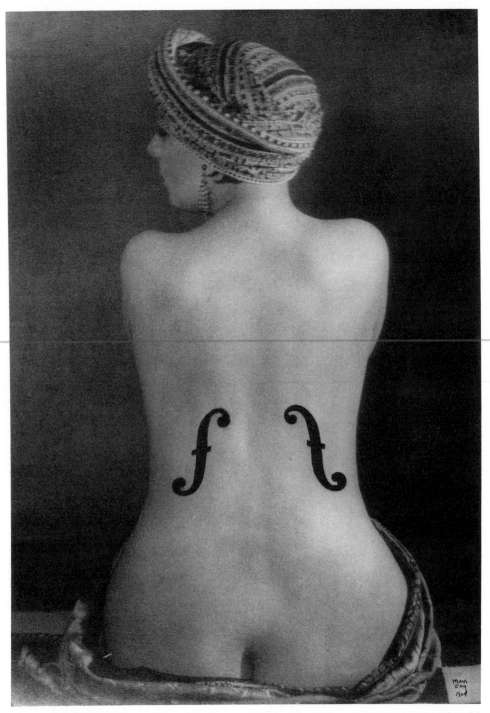

Photo Man Ray

KIKI IN MAN RAY'S CLASSIC 1924 IMAGE, *VIOLON D'INGRES*

NOTES AND COMMENTS

FOREWORD

p. 10 *Man Ray*   Among them are: Man Ray, *Self Portrait*; Brassai, *The Secret Paris of the '30s*; Djuna Barnes, "The Models Have Come to Town" in *Charm Magazine*; Robert McAlmon and Kay Boyle, *Being Geniuses Together*, 1920-1930; Morley Callaghan, *That Summer in Paris*; Samuel Putnam, *Paris Was Our Mistress*; and others like, Sisley Huddleston, *Back to Montparnasse*; John Glassco, *Memoirs of Montparnasse*; Charles Douglas, *Artist Quarter*; J.P. Crespelle, *Montparnasse Vivant*.

p. 10 *Shakespeare*   The original Shakespeare and Company was run by Sylvia Beach on rue de l'Odéon from 1919 to 1941. George Whitman opened his book store at 37, rue de la Bucherie on the Seine in 1951 and named it Shakespeare and Company in 1964, shortly after Beach's death. Mme. André, who had a book stall along the Seine, was shop-sitting that day.

p. 11 *Treize*   Her given name was Thérèse Maure, and in the 30s she married Manuel Cano de Castro. Many of the women we interviewed, took pseudonyms when they came to Montparnasse in order to remain anonymous from their more staid bourgeois families.

p. 16 *café life*   Artists' café life began in Montparnasse at the far ends of the boulevard du Montparnasse: Café de Versailles at place des Rennes across from Gare Montparnasse and the Closerie des Lilas at the eastern end of the boulevard at boulevard St. Michel. After the section of boulevard Raspail was opened north of boulevard du Montparnasse in 1904, the center of activity shifted to the cafés Le Dôme and La Rotonde at the intersection of boulevards Raspail and Montparnasse. Both cafés were originally filled with coachmen from the horse-drawn omnibuses that were stored on rue Delambre. Le Dôme attracted the relatively more affluent American and German artists. Kiki went to La Rotonde, whose owner from 1911, Victor Libion, became the most well-known of all the café owners that welcomed artists. Libion attracted an international mix of artists, models, writers,

KIKI AND MAN RAY RECALL GOYA'S *THE NAKED MAJA*

and even revolutionaries. André Salmon, critic, writer, and long-time resident of Montparnasse, suggested seriously that a statue of Libion should replace that of Balzac on boulevard Raspail just outside La Rotonde, and the stories Kiki tells suggest he deserved this honor.

p. 19 *celebrated*   One of the indications of the stable nature of their relationship was that when Kiki appeared in the film *Les Galerie des Monstres*, in 1924, she was billed as Kiki Ray.

p. 19 *wonder*   Both these letters to Man Ray are undated, but by internal evidence they were written in March 1922.

p. 22 Paris *Tribune*   The English language newspaper, the *Chicago Tribune, European Edition*, was familiarly known as the Paris *Tribune*. Its columns were written by different American writers living in Paris and chronicled the goings on in Montparnasse at the time. The report on Kiki's opening was found in Man Ray's papers and appeared in the "In the Quarter" column. It was undated, but by internal evidence appeared in March 1927.

p. 26 *Titus*   In 1924 Edward Titus moved to a small apartment over his rare-book shop at 4, rue Delambre around the corner from Le Dôme. In 1926 he began At the Sign of The Black Manikin Press to publish books by English-language writers and poets, illustrated by artists of the Quarter. In 1928 he took over the literary magazine, *This Quarter*, and continued to publish new poetry, fiction, and criticism by the English and American writers until 1932.

p. 29 *Putnam*   Samuel Putnam was a journalist and translator who had been working as editor with Titus on his magazine, *This Quarter*. He had translated Jean Cocteau, *Les Enfants terribles*; Joseph Delteil, *On the River Amour*; François Mauriac, *The Desert of Love*, as well as the works of Rabelais.

p. 29 *Memoirs*   The English edition was printed with the same text layout and format as the French edition, but on better paper. It has 14 more pages of text than the original French edition. This current edition is not a facsimile, but we have tried to keep the look and flavor of the original edition as designed by Henri Broca.

p. 30 *preceded her* In particular, we found a clipping in Bennett Cerf's papers at Columbia University from an article in *The New York World* by its literary editor Harry Hansen, who had somehow procured a copy of the memoirs and wrote, "They have given me a very good time and made me understand why Paris was tickled—or outraged—by them a year or more ago. Kiki's humor is certainly unconscious; it rests upon a complete lack of innuendo and subterfuge, an unexpected frankness about things that most people cover up." He reported that there were "about five copies" of *Kiki's Memoirs* in New York and predicted that the only way more copies would get into the country "is by way of the ship's steward, labeled Scotch." Titus obviously saw the article, because he wrote Cerf on September 11, "Too bad the stuff was not in New York before Hansen wrote his review. A thousand copies could have been sold easily the day after the appearance of the review. Why didn't you have sufficient courage to order them when you were here?" All the quotes come from the Titus-Cerf correspondence at Columbia University.

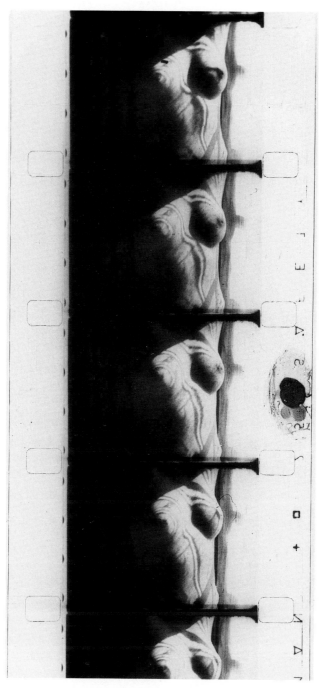

Man Ray, 1923

KIKI IN MAN RAY'S FIRST FILM, *RETURN TO REASON*, 1923

p. 32 *1929*   Man Ray, Aragon and Péret had been
asked by the editor of the Belgian Surrealist magazine
Variétés to contribute a manuscript that could be used to
raise money for the debt-plagued magazine. They came
up with *1929*. Printed in Belgium, it was immediately
seized by French customs on its way to Paris.

p. 34 *nightlife*   An American journalist visiting
Paris in 1931 remembers Kiki at The Jockey, "The orchestra, made up of American Negroes, was taking time
out for refreshment, and Kiki was leaning against the piano, singing without accompaniment. At the end of each
verse, she would stop and sip her drink, while the audience rendered the chorus. This consisted of chanting,
'Aaaaah, aah, ah,' until Kiki felt strong enough to re-
sume. Several times she attempted to stroll off to her
table, but on each occasion the crowd roared, 'Bis,
Bis!'(Again! Again!) until she returned and took up the
song."(Don Calhoun, "The Latin Quarter's Famous Kiki
Writes Her Memoirs," *St. Louis Post Dispatch*, February
8, 1931.)

p. 35 *newspaper*   The articles appeared as "Kiki

vous parle sans pose," in *Ici Paris Hebdo*, July 31, August 7, and August 14, 1950.

p. 38 *impulsively* The American writer Djuna Barnes, in an article on artists' models in Montparnasse, told the story this way, "Man Ray gives Kiki the credit for one of his best marines. She stormed into the room, so dark, so bizarre, so perfidiously willful crying, 'Never again will Kiki do the identical same thing three days running, never, never, never!' that in a flash he became possessed of the knowledge of all unruly nature." (Barnes, "The Models Have Come to Town," *Charm*, No. 4 [November 1924].)

MY FRIEND KIKI

Tsuguharu Foujita was born in Tokyo in 1886 to a family from the Samurai class. Foujita studied with a painter who had been in Paris in the 1880s. Although he had some success in Japan, in June 1913 Foujita persuaded his father to allow him to leave and arrived in Paris after a forty-five day sea voyage. He soon became a familiar part of the artists' community with his fringe haircut, eyeglasses, and earring. He married the painter Fernande Barrey in 1917 but left her in 1922, when he fell in love with Lucie Badoul, whom he christened Youki, "pink snow." Despite some early years of hardship, by the mid-1920s Foujita was an extremely successful painter. He showed in each annual Salon d'Automne and had yearly exhibitions at fashionable Right Bank galleries.

p. 41 *Winter* Kees Van Dongen in 1929 was an extremely successful painter, well known for his alluring portraits of society women. In 1922 he moved to a private house at 5 rue Juliet Lamber in the 17th arrondissement, where he hosted receptions attended by "tout-Paris."

p. 41 *Summer* Moïse Kisling, a painter who had been in Montparnasse since arriving from Poland in 1910, divided his time between his studio in Paris and the house he and his wife, Renée, and their two sons, Jean and Guy, rented in the south of France close to Sanary-sur-Mer.

p. 41 *studio* Foujita painted in a former stable in the courtyard of the apartment building where he lived

Jaque Catelain, 1924

KIKI DANCES IN THE CIRCUS PARADE IN THE 1924 FILM *GALERIE DES MONSTRES*

with painter Fernande Barrey, at 5 rue Delambre, just around the corner from Le Dôme.

p. 42 *nude*   To have been nude under her coat was Kiki's straightforward way of solving a problem that models I interviewed told me about—lines left by the elastics bands in their underwear.

p. 42 *her drawing*   This drawing, reproduced in the *Memoirs*, was in the collection of Henri Pierre Roché, who until John Quinn's death in 1924 acted as Quinn's agent in buying works by Picasso, Douanier Rousseau, and Brancusi. He was a fan of Kiki's work and bought several of her paintings and drawings. He planned to organize an exhibition of her works in 1925, but this never happened, due perhaps to the untimely death of Quinn.

p. 42 *Nu couchée*   The painting is *Nu Couché à la Toile de Jouy*, shown at the Salon d'Automne in 1922 and now in the collection of the Musée d'Art Moderne de la Ville de Paris.

p. 44 *for the State*   Foujita refers to the fact that the French government actively supported artists by buying works from the annual Salons.

p. 52 *The Enormous Room* e.e. cummings' book, published in 1922, dealt with his experiences as a prisoner in a French detention camp during the war.

p. 52 *Julian Green* "A popular Montparnassian," Green was a French writer born in Paris in 1900 of parents from the American south. His first novel was published in Paris in 1926, followed by two others in 1927 and 1929, all dealing with passion, pleasure, sin, and guilt.

p. 53 *the only one* Hemingway did in fact write another introduction, for *This Must Be the Place*, the memoirs of Jimmie Charters, a former boxer from Liverpool and the barman at the Dingo on rue Delambre, where Hemingway had been a regular.

They would go to boxing matches together; or when Hemingway had gone alone, "he would come to the bar afterward to tell me what he had seen. He would get so excited, sometimes, he would start sparring in the bar and almost knock someone over." (Charters)

p. 53 *Defoe* Hemingway is referring to Daniel Defoe's *Moll Flanders*.

A NOTE ON KIKI . . .

p. 55 *The vulgate* St. Jerome, Christian ascetic and scholar, lived from 342 to 420. After studying in Rome, and spending four years of intensive study in the remote Syrian desert, he moved to Bethlehem, where he revised the Gospels from the Old Latin and made a new Latin translation of the Psalms and the Old Testament from Greek and Hebrew sources. His work formed the basis of what became known as the Vulgate, or authorized Latin text of the Bible.

KIKI'S MEMOIRS

p. 75 *traipsed off* Unwed mothers were not tolerated in small towns and were forced to leave for Paris, often to work in maternity hospitals like Baudelocque to scare them from getting pregnant again.

p. 80 *next door* Maxime Legros' coal and charcoal shop was just down the street from Kiki's grandmother's house on rue de la Charme. He was a romantic figure who made charcoal in large open-air charring stacks in the

KIKI'S IMAGE FRAGMENTED BY A "VORTOSCOPE" IN *BALLET MÉCANIQUE*

forests above Châtillon and delivered it to surrounding towns, announcing his arrival with a silver trumpet.

p. 80 *six years*　While we do not know when Marie Prin left for Paris, and it is true that her relationship with Maxime Legros had been going on since 1898 when she was sixteen, it is unlikely that they ever lived together. One of Kiki's memories in her later article (p. 199) indicates that perhaps her mother stayed in Châtillon for a few years after Kiki was born and left when it became clear that Maxime Legros would not marry her. He did not marry until 1905, when he wed a farmer's daughter, Julie Jomin, from nearby Coulmier-le-Sec.

p. 81 *learn to read*　Marie Prin sent Kiki to the school on rue Vaugirard, around the corner from their apartment on rue Dulac, to improve her spelling so she could become a linotypist, as Kiki mentions on page 209.

Marie Prin lived in a ground floor apartment facing the courtyard in a building owned by the publishing house of Calmann Levy, for whom she worked as a linotypist. She made a stable life for herself and aspired to petit-bourgeois respectability.

p. 85 *quit school*   As soon as Kiki turned thirteen—the legal age at which children could begin work in factories— her mother took her out of school and sent her to work.

p. 85 *knitter's apprentice*   in French brocheuse, which more correctly is "book binder."

p. 86 *barely enough*   Although Marie Prin worked steadily as a linotypist, wages for women were so low that she remained poor. Before the war the average salary of working women was 2.25 francs for ten hours of work, whereas men earned more than 3 times as much, 7.78 francs per day.

p. 86 *hash joint*   In French, *soupe populaire*, a type of very inexpensive restaurant for workers that served only soup and existed in Paris until the 1950s.

p. 96 *job with a baker-lady*   In early 1916, Kiki's mother met a wounded soldier, Noel Delecoeuillerie, eleven years younger than herself, whom she married in January 1918. Possibly because of lack of space in the apartment on rue Dulac or jealousy of her young daughter, Marie found a new place for Kiki to live.

p. 102 *not far* Before World War I, most artists' models were Italian, as posing in the nude was not considered a respectable profession by the more prudish French. Often prostitutes saw themselves as a higher class than models. However at the beginning of the war the French government sent all of the Italian models back to Italy. The scarcity of professional models and more open social mores removed this prejudice, and modeling was a way young women living on their own in Montparnasse could earn money.

p. 104 *concert Mayol* A music-hall founded by a popular singer and performer Felix Mayol, it was similar to Folies-Bergere, with extravagenat production numbers featuring nude women.

p. 106 *Fratellini* The Fratellini brothers were the leading clowns at Cirque Médrano on boulevard de Rochechouart in Montmartre. The two clowns were friends of the artists, and Alexander Calder once made a mechanical dog for them to use in their act.

p. 110 *doing the pave* In French, *faire le trottoir*, translates as a "street walker."

Man Ray, 1928

KIKI STARRED IN *ÉTOILE DE MER*

p. 114 *pave*   Again, a prostitute.

p. 122 *Americans were camping*   The Americans came into the war in 1917.

p. 124 *Soutine*   Chaim Soutine grew up in extreme poverty in a village outside Minsk. He studied art in Minsk and later at the Academy of Fine Arts in Vilna, before coming to Paris in the summer of 1913 with his friend Michel Kikoïne. They are said to have walked across Paris from the Gare de l'Est directly to La Rotonde to meet fellow artists.

p. 124 *Cité Falguière*   Cité Falguière was a cluster of rudimentary one- and two-story artist studio buildings along an impasse that ran off rue Falguière, on the west side of Gare Montparnasse, not far from Kiki's mother's apartment. Modigliani had a studio there on the ground floor at No. 14 from 1910 to 1913, and Soutine moved into a studio in the same building around 1916.

p. 126 *burning*   Foujita tells the same story about his first visit to Fernande Barrey's studio.

p. 126 *three-toed shoes*   This probably means shoes

several sizes too large. Kiki describes some shoes she had in a later chapter.

p. 127 *It took* The French reads *"J'allaie timidement risquer deux sous aux appareils pour gagner de quoi prendre café et croisssant,"* which translates, "I went in shyly to risk a couple of *sous* in the slot machines to earn enough for coffee and croissant." People we interviewed told us that they remembered the slot machines in the bars at that time.

p. 128 See page 223 for more details about this hat.

p. 129 *Rosalie's* Rosalie Tobia was an Italian model who posed for years for the academic painter William Bouguereau. By 1906 she had grown too old to pose for nudes, so she took over a small crémerie at 3, rue Campagne Première that seated about twenty-four people, and fed "her" artists hearty Italian meals. Like many of the stores and restaurants in Montparnasse, Rosalie's readily gave artists credit when they were without money and sometimes allowed them to tack drawings on the wall as payment.

p. 130 *Modigliani*   Modigliani was Rosalie's favorite diner, but dramatic fights between them would erupt from time to time. They shouted Italian insults, broke dishes, and tore drawings off the wall. These fights were brief, and afterward they would calm down, embrace, and Modigliani would make new drawings for the walls.

p. 130 *good-looking*   *Mais qu'il était beau!* translates as "But how beautiful he was!"

p. 130 *Utrillo*   Maurice Utrillo lived with his mother, the painter Suzanne Valadon, and her husband André Utter, at 12 rue Cortot. It was at the top of the hill around the corner from the famous café Lapin Agile, which was the central meeting point for artists in Montmartre. As often as he could sneak away, Utrillo would join Modigliani at Chez Rosalie. They enjoyed drinking together, until Utrillo's mother appeared and took him home.

p. 132 *keeping house*   In 1918 Kiki fell in love with Maurice Mendjizky, a Polish painter, and lived with him for almost four years. In a Salon catalog for 1921 his studio is listed at 17, rue de Perceval, a block that is now torn down. The critic and poet André Salmon remembers, "she held the double job of model and mistress of a Polish painter. I went to the studio to see the artist's painting. I found a thin little gamine in a flowered dressing gown made of cheap material. Crouching in front of the fire that was refusing to catch, the little darling was blowing on it with all her heart and with all her faith in the painter before he had been reviewed in a major newspaper. So many sincere wishes were formed whilst she blew, her lips shaped as if she were playing a clarinet, her bottom in the air."

p. 132 *Potin*   A chain of grocery stores in Paris. When customers bought table wine, they brought back the old bottles which were rinsed and reused.

p. 133 *felon*   Small abscess on the finger, especially on or near the nail.

p. 133 *hundred years*   In French, C'est la dèche!, translates as "I'm completely broke!"

p. 136 *Husson*   Paul Husson managed to publish two issues of his monthly art and literary magazine *Montparnasse* before the outbreak of the war in 1914 forced him to suspended publication. The first post-war issue appeared on July 1, 1921. For the next two years, the café du Parnasse was its headquarters. Kiki's chronology is off by about one year.

p. 136 *show my bosom*   Secure about her position in the artists' community, Kiki could turn what was traumatic for her as a teenager into a performance and a joke.

p. 136 *Parnasse Bar*   Café du Parnasse was located next to La Rotonde, which absorbed it in 1924.

p. 136 *pictures*   It was a practice, starting with café du Parnasse, which printed a catalogue and announcements, to exhibit works by Montparnasse artists on the walls of the cafés.

p. 136 Brosset   Victor Libion sold La Rotonde in 1920.

p. 139 *Kisling*   Kisling became successful very quickly. His openness, generosity, and good spirits made him one of the most visible and popular people in Montparnasse, and his studio was one of the centers of social activity.

KIKI, *NUDES*, 1925

p. 142 *contract*   There are no traces of such contracts between artists and models. However, Kisling, like many other artists, had models he liked and would use them over and over again.

p. 142 *Zborowski*   A young Polish poet turned art dealer, Leopold Zborowski was Modigliani's dealer and protector from 1917 until Modigliani's death in 1920. He was also Soutine's dealer. Zborowski and his wife lived on the floor below Kisling's studio at 3 rue Joseph Bara.

p. 143 *Fels*   Florent Fels was an art critic and good friend of Kisling.

p. 147 *forty-sous piece*   The old measurement of money based on increments of 20. There were 20 sous to a franc, so a 40-sous piece was equivalent to 2 francs.

p. 148 *an American*   In his memoirs, titled Self Portrait, Man Ray remembers their meeting: "I was sitting in a café one day, chatting with Marie Vassilieff. . . . Across the room sat two young girls. . . . The prettier one waved a greeting to Marie, who told me it was Kiki, a favorite model. . . . Marie invited Kiki and her friend to sit down at our table." They went to the movies, where Man

Ray "hardly looked at the screen and sought Kiki's hand in the dark."

Man Ray asked Kiki to pose for him. She hesitated, saying that photographs would reveal her "physical defect." Man Ray persisted, and finally Kiki agreed, and they went to his attic room on rue La Condamine. "Kiki got undressed behind a screen in the corner and came out, modestly holding her hand in front of her, exactly like Ingre's painting of La Source. Looking at her from head to foot I could see no physical defect. She smiled shyly like a little girl and said that she had no pubic hairs." She told him that "she had tried everything, pomades, massage, nothing worked." Man Ray assured her, "that was fine, it would pass the censors."

"I got her to take a few poses, concentrating on her head; I soon gave up . . . other thoughts surged in. I told her to dress and we went out to the café." The next day, "I showed Kiki the prints when she came. She was duly impressed. . . . Presently she undressed while I sat on the edge of the bed with the camera before me. When she came out from behind the screen, I motioned to her to come and sit beside me. I put my arms around her, she did the same; our lips met, and we both lay down. No pictures were taken that afternoon."

p. 148 *La Dame aux Camelias*   *Camille*, made in the United States in 1921, was a modern-dress version of Alexandre Dumas' famous novel and play, starring Rudolph Valentino and Alla Nazimova. It was not shown in France until January 1, 1923, at the Electric Palace on boulevard des Italiens, long after Kiki and Man Ray were lovers.

p. 148 *Vassilieff*   Marie Vassilieff, a tiny, energetic Russian artist and long-time resident of Montparnasse, who had come to Paris in 1907, studied at the Matisse Academy and was part of the Russian artists' group at the Rotonde. She held drawing classes in her studio on avenue de Maine just before the war and ran an artists' canteen there during the war. Abandoning painting, she made elegant and very detailed leather portrait dolls.

p. 149 *something to eat*   These were restaurants in the Quarter. Man Ray notes "We had full meals every day . . . she began to put on weight, which did not bother her, and was delighted when some pubic hair began to appear." Still Kiki could joke about her "defect" as Man Ray relates: "One night at a gay party at Foujita's, she impersonated Napoleon. Putting on a hat sideways, she lifted her dress to her waist and stuck a hand into her bosom. Her white thighs (she wore no drawers) were a perfect replica of the emperor's white breeches. Everyone roared with laughter and applauded." (All quotes from Man Ray come from his *Self Portrait*, published by Little, Brown and Company in 1963 and reissued in 1989.)

p. 149 *in the hotel room* In early December 1921, four months after he arrived in Paris, Man Ray moved into room No. 37 at the Hotel des Écoles, on rue Delambre, where Kiki joined him. In order to support himself with his photography, Man Ray arranged his hotel room into a studio. Gertrude Stein came there to be photographed and noted, "I have never seen any space . . . so admirably disposed. He had a bed, he had three large cameras, he had several kinds of lighting, he had a window screen and in a little closet he did all of his developing." Eventually Man Ray photographed most of the English and American writers in Paris. He also photographed artists and their works, including Picasso, Braque, Gris, and Matisse. He became increasingly successful and photographed more artists, writers, visiting Americans, and European aristocracy. In 1922 he moved with Kiki to a new studio at 31 bis rue Campagne Première.

p. 149 *Dadaists*   The artists Kiki names were members of the Paris Dadaists group, the leaders of whom were Tristan Tzara and Francis Picabia. Man Ray, who arrived from New York in 1921, was introduced to the group by Marcel Duchamp and was the only American artist to become part of the French art community. The Dadaists arranged for an exhibition of Man Ray's paintings and objects in December 1921. By 1924 André Breton had left the Dadaist group and formulated the ideas that became Surrealism. Man Ray also became an accepted member of the Surrealists, who were enthusiastic over his photographs, rayographs, and experimental films.

p. 149 *don't see much difference*   Man Ray found the same similarity, at least as it came to painting. When he

Photo Man Ray

KIKI AND HER FRIEND LILI BEHIND GIACOMETTI'S *THE PALACE AT 2 A.M.*

showed his work at the Galerie Surréaliste in 1926, he noted, "aside from two or three works I created since the birth of the new movement, I again showed my things of the Dada period. They fitted in just as well with the Surrealist idea."

p. 149 *bore me* Man Ray writes: "I did take Kiki with me sometimes to the cafés of my more intellectual friends, or to their homes. She was perfectly at ease and amused everyone with her quips, but got bored if the conversation became too abstract for her. Unlike the wives or mistresses of the others, who tried to keep up with the current or kept silent, she became restless; I took her back to her beloved Montparnasse . . . Kiki told me some of my most intellectual friends had propositioned her."

p. 151 *black race* In his memoirs written in 1963, Man Ray comments on this passage: "Referring to my portraits, she observed a certain lack of logic on my part. I had criticized her penchant for bright, gaudy colors, yet I had photographed some of the Negro cast from the Blackbirds musical that was taking Paris by storm.

Therefore, I did like color, she argued." Somewhat prudishly he adds, "Except in referring to me as her lover, the rest of the chapter was discreet, as were other references to me in the book."

p. 153 *The Jockey*   The chronology in the *Memoirs* is incorrect; Kiki went to New York in the summer of 1923 and returned to Montparnasse just before the opening of The Jockey in November of that year.

p. 153 *Hilaire Hiler*   A self-taught painter born in 1898 in St. Paul, Minnesota, Hiler had a studio on rue Broca and was part of Montparnasse artistic and social life from the early 1920s until he returned to the U.S. in the mid-1930s. He also decorated the nightclub La Jungle. He wrote books on the history of costume and color theory in painting.

p. 153 *The Jockey*   The nightclub opened on the site of an old wine store, painted by Utrillo, on boulevard du Montparnasse at the corner of rue Campagne Première, just down the street from Man Ray's studio. In 1921 it became Le Caméléon, a restaurant that served the artists inexpensive meals of sauerkraut and sausages and

KIKI, *THE TIGHTROPE WALKER*, 1927

became a literary and artistic meeting place. Programs included literary evenings, musical performances, and, on Sundays, humorists, who vigorously insulted the audience.

There was a long wooden bar, tables around the wall, and a tiny dance floor. Hiler painted figures of Mexicans, cowboys, and Indians on the exterior and installed an electric sign.

The artists immediately made the Jockey their place.

p. 154 *Daddy Londish* M. and Mme. Londish had been the owners of the Le Caméléon, and took The Jockey over after a few years.

p. 154 *Florianne* American writer Robert McAlmon described Florianne's dancing: "She was doing an Eastern dance, writhing her long-waisted hipless body. Her small, firm breasts swayed back and forth as she bent backwards to the floor, her arms weaving, her sensitive mouth lovely with intensity and emotion" (McAlmon, *Being Geniuses Together*).

p. 155 *don't mean* Putnam has changed the meaning by inserting "I don't mean." The French *en talon* translates as "in stocking feet."

p. 155 *the sh—* In French *des . . . emmerdeuses.*

p. 157 *Per Krohg* A Norwegian painter who grew up in Montparnasse, lived with his wife Lucy and son Guy in a studio in the same building as Kisling. In 1920 Lucy fell in love with the painter Jules Pascin, but their affair did not become known until about 1925, when Per and Guy moved alone to a new studio on rue Val de Grace. Per fell in love with Thérèse Treize.

p. 157 *Derain* André Derain was a leading member of the Fauvist group of painters and was a close neighbor and friend of Vlaminck, Picasso, and Braque in Montmartre. In 1910 he left Montmartre and moved to a studio at 10 rue Bonaparte near Montparnasse, where he became good friends with Kisling. His work was exhibited widely in Paris and abroad during this period, and he designed sets and costumes for a number of ballets for the Ballets Russes and other companies. He was considered a maitre by the painters in Montparnasse and a welcome part of their social life.

p. 157 *Ivan Mosjoukine*. Born in 1889, Ivan Mosjoukine was one of the leading actors in Russian silent films. After the revolutions in 1917 he emigrated to Paris.

Kiki and Mosjoukine were lovers for a brief time. Treize remembers that he came to look for Kiki and Treize at The Jockey. "He drove fast in his sports car, was a charmer, a seducer, and also a simple person. He spoke French fairly well. Kiki went to see Mosjoukine at his place in a bachelor hotel. Kiki and Mosjoukine were like beautiful cats together. His wife was jealous, but she was not there."

p. 157 *Jaque Catelain*   He was a well-known leading man in French silent films, but in 1923 he wrote, directed, and starred in *La Galerie des Monstres*. According to Treize, he came to The Jockey and rounded up people to have bit parts in the film. See below for more details on Kiki's role in the film.

p. 157 *what gowns*   There is an additional sentence in the French edition that is not in the English translation: "I don't know any other place now except for La

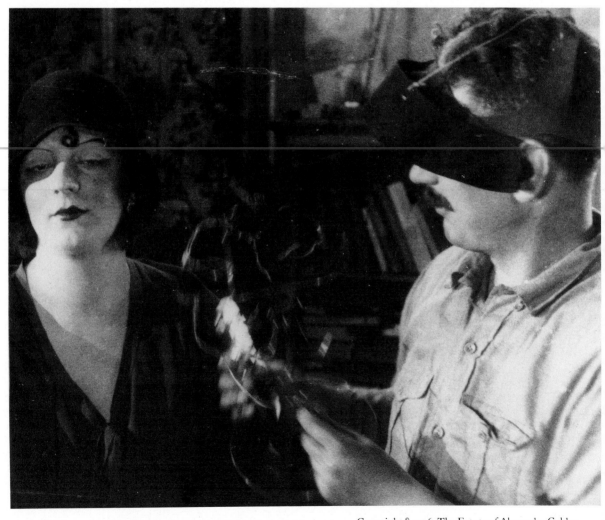

CALDER ASKED KIKI TO POSE FOR HIM
WHEN A NEWSREEL CREW FILMED HIM

Jungle where you can have that much fun and still be so completely natural."

p. 158 *New York*   The full circumstances of Kiki's trip to New York are still not known. According to Man Ray, "Kiki brought a couple to my studio . . . They were Americans touring Europe looking for talent. The man was tall and handsome, the woman somewhat older than he; they seemed affluent. They were enchanted by Kiki, her singing and personality, and suggested taking her to the States where they were sure they could get her a contract in the theater or the movies. All expenses would be taken care of. She would be placed with a French family in Greenwich Village . . . they'd protect her. . . . I was persuaded, gave my approval. . . . There were tearful farewells at the boat train. . . . I gave her a couple of addresses of friends, including my sister."

But Treize told us a different story. During the summer of 1923 Kiki met Mike, an American journalist from a St. Louis newspaper. Mike was, as Treize reports, "handsome and a good lover . . . and it was a marvelous, sensual encounter. He was happy with Kiki, called her 'mon petit haricot blanc,' and they made good love together."

One of the strains in Kiki's relationship with Man Ray was that she felt Man Ray was undemonstrative and cold. Treize said that Kiki decided to leave Man Ray as a result of a specific incident: "Sitting at dinner, Kiki said to Man Ray, 'Man I love you,' to which he answered, 'Love, what's that, imbecile? We don't love, we screw.'" Kiki decided Man Ray didn't love her and left for New York with Mike. They stayed at the Hotel Lafayette in Greenwich Village. Someone did arrange an appointment for her at the Paramount studios in Astoria, Queens, but nothing came of it.

We never were able to locate a journalist named Mike, but a hint of his existence came in an article about Kiki by Don Calhoun which appeared in the February 8, 1931, issue of the *St. Louis Post-Dispatch*. He wrote that his "acquaintance with Kiki was brought about through the chap who persuaded her to make her American film venture. He wanted a letter delivered to her."

The date of the trip, from around the end of July to October 1923, was established by a letter from Man Ray to his sister Elsie, dated September 30, 1923, "I just got a letter today from Kiki. If you haven't yet seen her, go to

ONE OF THREE KNOWN POSES WITH BAOULÉ MASK

61 Washington Square, care of Palmers. Tell me exactly what is passing as near as you can find out discreetly." We were never able to discover who the Palmers were.

Kiki also visited Man Ray's family in Brooklyn. His sister, Dorothy Ray Goodbread, whom Kiki called "Mme. Bon Pain," found Kiki "a friendly, happy, bubbly person, a blithe spirit." She remembered that during an outing, Kiki led the whole family along Kosciusko Boulevard, waving a soup ladle as a baton, singing the Marseillaise.

p. 161 *cups*   The wine was probably served in coffee cups because of Prohibition.

p. 161 *Paramount*   A gossip item in the Paris *Tribune* in July 12, 1924, referred to Kiki's trying out for the movies: "The Montparnasse cut-up went to New York last season to have a try at the American film, but as she spoke no English, she suddenly got panicky and came back to Paris."

p. 161 *Galerie des Monstres*   The film by Jaque Catelain was set in a traveling circus in Spain. Kiki, listed in the credits as "Kiki Ray," played herself, Kiki de Mont-

Photo Man Ray

IN A SECOND POSE KIKI HOLDS THE BAOULÉ MASK TO HER FACE

parnasse, as did Florence Martin, a former dancer with the Hoffman Girls, and the dwarf, Le Tarare, and two models Bronia and Tylia Perlmutter.

Catelain and a fifteen-year-old American, Lois Moran, in her film debut, play two young Spaniards (Ralda and Riquette) who flee their families, marry, and join the circus, run by an animal trainer named Buffalo. The circus comes to Toledo and there is a parade, in which each performer does a small bit: Kiki, Flossie Martin, Le Tarare, and Tylia and Bronia Perlmutter perform in this sequence. Buffalo makes advances to Ralda who spurns him. In anger, he frees the lion, who attacks and badly hurts Ralda. Buffalo forces Riquette to perform while Ralda lies wounded. After the performance, the other circus people help the lovers flee the circus and make a new start in life. The shooting did not go smoothly. When the lion refused to act ferocious, Catelain offered it a live rabbit. The rabbit scared the lion, and they had to fake the attack scene.

p. 161 *three months*   According to Treize, Mike had to return to St. Louis. He left Kiki with some money.

Photo Man Ray

MAN RAY CALLED THIS POSE *NOIRE ET BLANCHE*, AND IT APPEARED IN *VOGUE PARIS*, MAY

Alone and frightened, she went to the movies every day. Finally, she wired Man Ray for help.

Man Ray continues his story: "One morning there was a cable—an S.O.S. asking me to send her the fare for her return. I complied at once and received a wire telling me when her boat would arrive. I took the train to Le Havre and met her as she landed. . . . She was happy now, was not interested in a career, would stay with me forever. In the train on the way back to Paris, we sat silently holding hands as in the movies on our first encounter." But a few days later Kiki stormed up to Man Ray on a café terrace and accused him of having an affair with one of her friends while she was away and then gave him "a resounding slap." They went to Hotel Istria where "she continued to call me names. I hit her so hard she fell on the bed. Rolling over, she ran to a table near the window, picked up a bottle of ink and threw it at me, but it hit the wall . . . she then broke the window with her fist, opened wide the casement, screaming murder and threatened to jump if I approached her. The maid came in , followed by the proprietor, who ordered us to leave at once, demanding indemnity for the damage to the room.

When they left we fell into each other's arms. Kiki weeping and I laughing. We moved to another hotel."

p. 162 *American sailors*   Villefranche was reserved for foreign military ships visiting the Mediterranean and was full of American sailors from the S.S. Pittsburgh on a goodwill mission to France.

p. 166 *fell over arms first*   Kiki's version may not have been exactly accurate. In his memoirs, Man Ray relates that when the two officers appeared at the Welcome hotel and requested that Kiki follow them, "She demanded an explanation, whereat one of the men seized her by the arm, calling her an ugly name. She picked up her hand bag and swung it into his face."

p. 167 *showed me the goldfish for fair*   In French, *m'en raconte de toutes les couleurs*, which translates as "insulted me in the most graphic language possible."

p. 171 *gentleman friend*   When Man Ray found out Kiki was in jail, he and Treize immediately enlisted the help of all their friends. Robert Desnos contacted Georges Malkine, the surrealist painter, who was temporarily working in Nice. His correspondence with Desnos gives a full account of his efforts to free Kiki.

p. 171 *lawyer*   Malkine also found that Kiki's court-appointed lawyer, Bonifacio, "did not believe a word of Kiki's story," thinking her a quarrelsome Parisian prostitute. A letter from Malkine's boss, the head of the largest garbage-disposal company in Nice, convinced the lawyer to help Kiki. For the most serious charge of hitting a police officer, Bonifacio made a visit to the accusing police commissioner, whom he knew, and procured a more "benign" statement.

p. 175 *gentleman friend*   Man Ray hurried to Nice with a medical report from Dr. Theodore Fraenkel—a doctor who was a collector and friend of the Montparnasse artists—that Kiki was high-strung, and with depositions from Desnos and Louis Aragon that she was a serious artist.

Just before the trial, Malkine wrote Desnos: "The certificate of F[raenkel] was a very good thing. For the rest, I am not absolutely sure if your and Aragon's testimony can be useful. It's possible the judge could be gotten to di-

ON A SANDY BEACH

Photo Man Ray

rectly. In any case, it is possible to have an acquittal. . . .
Man Ray imagines that Bonifacio lacks brilliance. The
truth is that he is intentionally giving the least amount of
detail possible, because this judge, Niel, dishes out punishment according to the length of the arguments."

p. 174 *gazebo* In French, *bandit*, translates as
crook.

p. 178 *free again* Unfortunately Kiki was not ac-
quitted; she received a two-month suspended sentence
with one to three years probation.

p. 179 *Ernest* Paul Chambon was the patron of Le
Dôme, and one of his sons was Ernest. Le Dôme was en-
larged and remodeled in 1928, and they opened a new
'bar Americain.'

p. 181 *Cocteau* Cocteau, with his infallible nose for
talent, discovered Man Ray soon after he arrived in
Paris and had his photo made with his cane and multicolored knitted gloves.

p. 183 *Boeuf* Early in 1921, Cocteau and his crowd
made a bar named the Gaya on rue Duphot so popular

and overcrowded that the manager Louis Moyses began to look for a larger space, which he found on rue Boissy d'Anglas. He used the name of Darius Milhaud's and Cocteau's ballet Le Boeuf sur le Toit. The Boeuf opened January 1922, and throughout the twenties it had the loudest jazz, the prettiest women, and the latest art-world gossip to be found in Paris. Picabia's paintings and Man Ray's photographs of Cocteau's crowd hung on the walls. The Montparnasse crowd went there regularly.

p. 183 *Doucet* Jean Wiéner was the pianist who asked his friend the Belgian Clement Doucet to take over some of the playing at the Boeuf. Doucet used to read and play at the same time.

p. 184 *necklace* This necklace can be seen in some of the photos of Kiki in 1929.

p. 187 *at the cafés* In the French edition Kiki mentions Le Dôme and the Select, on opposite sides of boulevard Montparnasse. The Select opened in 1925 and was the first café to stay open 24 hours a day. By the late 1920s, La Rotonde had fallen out of favor with Kiki's crowd.

Youki was Foujita's wife in 1929.

Koyonagi-Sessu-Hayakawa was the lover of Fernande Barrey at this time.

Fernande Barrey, an artist who was a long-time resident of Montparnasse, had been married to Foujita from about 1916 until he met Youki in 1922.

Lucy Krohg was still married to Per Krohg, but her love affair with Pascin was common knowledge, and she was no longer living with Per. She continued to appear to feed their son Guy dinner and send him off to school in the morning, but she spent most of her time with Pascin.

p. 188 *Man Ray* He comments on this passage, "she wrote of my artistic activities and my preoccupation with the bits of paper, hardware and cotton which went into the making of my Rayographs," which were created from objects or forms laid on light-sensitive paper and exposed to lights that Man Ray had arranged to fall on the paper from different angles and intensities. He even made a rayograph of himself kissing Kiki.

p. 189 *Coupole* The large restaurant with dancing in the basement was located on boulevard Montparnasse just down from Le Dôme It opened in December 1927 and was an immediate sensation. The artists made the Coupole Bar their place. They would meet there before dinner and always ended up there for a last drink before heading home to bed.

p. 191 *dancing places*   There were not that many places that offered dancing. In addition to The Jockey, there was La Cigogne, La Coupole, La Jungle, and Le Parnasse on rue Delambre.

p. 191 *Foujita's*   Foujita and Youki lived in a luxurious house at Parc Montsouris. Desnos became a regular visitor to their house; he and Youki would stay up listening to records on an old Edison phonograph long after Foujita had gone to bed. Desnos gradually transferred his affections to Youki.

p. 191 *Mercadier and Paulus*   Mercadier and Paulus were singers from the turn of the century.

p. 191 *Pascin*   Pascin's generosity was legendary among his friends. When he was not working, Pascin was surrounded by people, at home or in the cafés. He invited people to Saturday night dinners and twenty or thirty

DURING HER EXHIBITION AT THE GALLERY AU SACRE DU PRINTEMPS, MARCH 1927

friends would gather in his studio on boulevard Clichy before going to their favorite restaurants. After-dinner festivities started with rounds of the nightclubs in Montmartre and Montparnasse, sometimes a visit to a favorite brothel, and could go on until dawn. Pascin gave parties in his studio, famous for tables laden with food and bottles of wine and for the open door to the street that admitted many more people than invited, many of them completely unknown to the host.

p. 191 *of all shades* One of Pascin's models and close friends was Julie Luce. Born in Martinique, she came to Paris in 1902 and was an actress and long-time resident of Montmartre.

p. 191 *Nils Dardel* A Swedish painter who lived in Montmartre on rue Lepic, he and his wife Thora were good friends of Pascin.

p. 192 *Bal* Costume balls were often sponsored by artists' groups to raise money for poorer artists. La Horde was a group whose headquarters were at La Rotonde. Bal Russe was probably organized by Russian artists who had long had an organization in Montparnasse.

p. 192 *Bal Suédois*   This annual ball was held at the Swedish cultural center Maison Watteau on rue Jules Chaplain in Montparnasse. Artists like Per Krohg, Nils Dardel, and Pascin made elaborate decorations for the yearly event. Kiki called it Académie Watteau because it did hold drawing and painting classes, where Per Krohg among others taught.

KIKI TALKS OPENLY TO YOU

p. 196 *father, 19*   According to his birth certificate, Maxime Legros was born in 1873 and thus was ten years older than Kiki's mother.

p. 197 *bed*   Kiki was born in her Grandmother's house at 9 rue de la Charme.

p. 198 *real Pernod*   One of the most poplar drinks at this time was absinthe. Because of bad reactions and deaths from drinking absinthe, it was eventually outlawed. Pernod, which had been making absinthe bottles, fashioned a less potent drink to take its place.

p. 199 *Six Reunited Bastards*   Kiki lists only five.

Madeleine's older sister Eugénie, mentioned in the *Memoirs*, may have been the sixth. She was older and may have left Châtillon early in Kiki's childhood

p. 202 *peute*   in Parisian argot *pute* meant prostitute, and Kiki was quick to point out the difference.

p. 204 *circumstances*   While it is true Marie Prin had two babies before Kiki, both of whom died shortly after birth, we found no evidence that foul play was involved.

p. 221 *Aicha*   While we have not been able to identify all these models, Aicha was a well-known model and personage in Montparnasse. She came from the north of France, joined the circus at age six, and became a bareback rider. At 16 she met Pascin and left for the freer life of Montparnasse.

p. 221 *Pâquerette*   Pâquerette, whose full name was Emilienne Pâquerette Geslot, was a clothes model for Paul Poiret and a regular at La Rotonde during the war years. She was one of Picasso's mistresses during 1916.

p. 272 *Calder asked Kiki*   Kiki had become such a famous celebrity that in 1928 the young American sculp-

Photo Mécano

KIKI TURNS WHAT COULD BE AN AWKWARD POSE
INTO A PROVOCATIVE IMAGE

tor, Alexander Calder, asked her to pose for him when Pathé newsreel filmed him making a wire sculpture portrait.

Memoirs   According to the Paris *Tribune*, Titus also displayed Kiki's paintings in his book shop on rue Delambre at the time of the publication of the memoirs.

Kiki's moods—she has a vast repertory—are expressed in the manner of doing her hair. When she is being the lady she wears a chignon. When it pleases her to appear a creature of mystery and romance she brushes her hair back in darkly shining wings, hiding her ears. When she is being Kiki it is geometrically banged and bobbed, which brings out the peculiarly feline quality of her eyes.

Thora Dardel's most vivid memory of Kiki was on the terrasse of Le Dôme, emptying the contents of the makeup case she always carried, and applying her makeup, using three or four colors of green to make her eyes match her dress.

Djuna Barnes described a rather dreamy Kiki on a café terrasse in her article for *Charm*: "'Life,' murmurs

Kiki, 'is *au fond*, so limited, so robbed of new sins, so *diabolique*' she raises her mandarin eyes, slanting with kohl 'that one must have a mouse, a small white mouse, *n'est-ce pas*? To run about between cocktails and *thé*.' Holding the little thing upon her rouged fingers, the favorite model of Montparnasse turns its warm dexterity toward the Boulevard Raspail, where, with sharp sparkling eyes it gazes on all men, without prejudice, knowing nothing of the comforts of 'good and evil.' A shade of the same concern is in the eyes of Kiki, who among other lovely women models, has come and conquered France. . . . and with it all they must have their fancies. For Kiki it is a white mouse. . . . Holding her white mouse in her hand, smiling her mandarin smile. 'They have broken my heart? Not at all, I keep it for me. What will you have, *thé*? *Bon*!'" (Barnes, 'The Models Have Come to Town," *Charm* 3, No. 4 [November 1924], 15; reprinted in Barnes, *Interviews*, 297-303.)

Cummings and a friend, William Slater Brown, were volunteers in Norton Hartjes Ambulance Corps attached to the French army. His friend wrote derogatory letters about the higher ups in the corps and was arrested by the

MAN RAY'S USE OF SHADOWS BECOMES MORE COMPLEX

nervous French censors. Cummings was accused of nothing more than being his close friend. They were held for more than 3 months at the Campe de Triage at La Ferté Macé in Normandy, awaiting the disposition of their cases. Cummings describes with youthful good spirits life in the detention camp: where he and his fellow inmates—about forty suspected spies of all nationalities—slept on straw mattresses, ate *soupe* from wooden bowls, and—except for two or three *promenades* per day in a small enclosed courtyard—spent all their waking time together in the Enormous Room of the title. Beneath the almost surreal depictions of the inmates and guards, the personal and physical suffering become painfully clear.

ABOUT THE EDITORS

Born in Monaco, Billy Klüver graduated from the Royal Institute of Technology, Stockholm, and received his Ph.D. from the University of California, Berkeley. Formerly a scientist at the Bell Telephone Laboratories, he has published numerous technical and scientific papers and holds ten patents. He has worked with such individual artists as Jean Tinguely, Robert Rauschenberg, Andy Warhol, Yvonne Rainer, and John Cage. In 1966, with Fred Waldhauer, Rauschenberg, and Robert Whitman, he founded Experiments in Art and Technology, an influential foundation that provides artists with access to new technology. The foundation has carried out more than 40 collaborative projects world-wide.

Dr. Klüver is co-author, with Julie Martin, of *Kiki's Paris*, a history of the Montparnasse art community from 1880 to 1930. *A Day with Picasso*, which has appeared in German and French editions, will be published in 1997.

Born in Nashville, Tennessee, Julie Martin (B.A. Philosophy, Radcliffe; M.A. Columbia) holds a Certificate from the Russian Institute of Columbia University. Her experience includes working as production assistant to artist Robert Whitman, and positions as researcher and associate producer at the Canadian Broadcasting Company, Ottawa, and at CBS-TV, New York, producing documentaries on contemporary art and the Soviet Union. She is on the staff of Experiments in Art and Technology, where she has served as editor of the newsletter. Together with Billy Klüver she wrote *Kiki's Paris* and is currently working with him on a social and art history of international art communities in the U.S., Western Europe, and Japan, 1945 to 1965.